THE SWIMMING POOL

Illustrations by
JOSEPH ESCOURIDO

THE SWIMMING POOL

BY ALICE COBB

FRIENDSHIP PRESS
NEW YORK

SPECIAL thanks are due to the staff members of Marcy Center, Newbury Avenue Center and Chicago Commons, in Chicago, particularly to Miss Mona Kewish, Mr. Hazzard S. Parks, Miss Berta Engle, Mr. Barrington Dunbar, and Mr. William Bruckman.

Thanks are also due to Mrs. Leola Harwell and her family, of Maywood, Illinois, whose home provided the background and some of the incidents for the story.

TO MY SISTER

CONTENTS

Preston Harlow shivered. It was cold out there on the front porch! No snow, because in Midwest Mayville it hardly ever snowed much after January. But the early February morning was cold—cold and raw!

The cheerful fire burning in the front room made the gray house warm inside, but outside all was bare, and the crab apple tree in the yard looked as if it were dead.

Preston shivered again and pulled his jacket closer. But he wasn't really thinking much about the weather as he looked anxiously up and down Fourth Place.

Where could Benjy Weinberg be? Could his father have taken him to the synagogue? Why didn't he come? Could Benjy have forgotten about today?

Surely not, because this was an especially special Saturday. Preston reached a dark hand into his pocket and pulled out the flier. There were the words in plain English:

GRAND OPENING—
NEW METROPOLIS SWIMMING POOL
Saturday, February 4, 10:00 A.M.
All Boys and Girls Welcome　　　15¢ *Admission*

He read the flier carefully all the way through and then felt in his pocket again to make sure the wallet was there. Fifteen cents for swimming and thirty cents for bus fare. Metropolis was eight miles from Mayville. Preston had never taken the bus ride alone to the city. Benjy had often, because he usually went to synagogue on Saturday mornings. Today Preston and Benjy were going together to the new swimming pool at Metropolis.

But where was Benjy?

Preston touched the neat little bundle under his arm, with the fresh towel folded in a square and the new red swimming trunks Mama had bought for him. He felt a warm glow of pride. Those new trunks were keen!

He heard a tap on the window behind him and turned around. Mama was there, smiling at him from inside. Mama's face was pretty—warm and brown and kind. He liked brown faces best, he thought. But she looked anxious now.

"Preston!" she called from behind the glass. "You'll take cold standing out there. Better come back in."

"Well—" he began. Just then he saw the Weinberg front door open down the street and a small figure come dashing out and down the sidewalk.

"Here comes Benjy!" Preston shouted. " 'Bye, Mama!"

"Preston, you're sure it said *all* boys and girls?" Her voice sounded worried.

"Oh, sure!" he answered. " 'Bye!"

He waved and ran down to meet Benjy. The day had begun!

Benjy was puffing when he reached Preston.

"Gee, I thought I'd never get away!" he exclaimed. "Hey, I bet you got new trunks! I just got old ones."

He held up his bundle, trunks and towel. Preston suddenly felt a little sorry for Benjy. Benjy was rich all right, but he didn't have new red trunks! And Benjy was rather short and nearsighted so that he had to wear glasses. But Benjy was his pal! Benjy was all right!

"Well, let's get going," Preston said importantly. He sometimes felt as if he had to look after Benjy. "Come on."

They started briskly down the street, Benjy just a little behind, still puffing when they reached the Anderson house and looked for Murf, who was usually hanging around. But Murf's house was shut up tight, and not a one of the eleven Anderson children was in sight. The yard looked shabby as always. Benjy kicked a tin can off the sidewalk.

"Looks like they could put their stuff in a trash can!"

he exclaimed. "Papa says it's a disgrace the way people are moving into our neighborhood and cluttering things up."

"He does?" Preston wasn't much interested.

"Yeah. He says there's no old families left here now except us and the Cotters, and Papa says maybe we'll just have to move ourselves if this keeps up."

"Gee, Benjy, I hope not!" Preston said. "I'd rather Joe Cotter would move than you!"

"Yeah, I don't like him much either," Benjy agreed. "He's too stuck-up. I reckon his mother wants to move, too, but they can't afford to, my papa says. He says moving is the *trend of the times!*"

"The—the what?" Preston was impressed.

"Trend of the times," Benjy repeated. "Papa says first it was nig—well, he says we're just getting all kinds of people on Fourth Place!"

Preston didn't notice Benjy's slip because he saw Mr. Huntington standing on the corner where the bus stopped. Mr. Huntington was the minister at Central Church where Preston and his mother went.

"Hi ya, Mr. Huntington!" he shouted. "Guess what! Benjy and I are going to Metropolis on the bus to the new swimming pool."

Mr. Huntington turned and saluted.

"You don't say so! Off to the big city, are you?"

Preston liked the way Mr. Huntington smiled. It was a little the way Mama smiled, except that of course Mr.

Huntington was white. All the people in Central Church were white except Preston's family.

"We're going to the opening of the new swimming pool," Benjy told Mr. Huntington. "It's for all boys and girls."

"Good!" Mr. Huntington said. "Are you sure it said *all?*"

"Yes, sir." Preston took the flier out and showed him.

Just then the big yellow bus pulled up to the bus stop.

"I guess this is your wagon," Mr. Huntington said. "Got your money ready? O.K. Up you go!" He gave each of them a little boost up the steps. Then he stood back and saluted again. "Good-by—and good swimming!"

The boys waved, paid their fare, and sat down on the empty front seat. The bus heaved and moved on.

"Gee, he's nice!" Benjy observed. "Seems to like you."

"He likes everybody," Preston exclaimed. "And everybody likes him, too. He's a right guy. Why don't you come to our church sometime?"

"Well—" Benjy hesitated. "Papa wouldn't like it. He says it's all right to do business with Christians, but nothing else. He says Christians and Jews oughtn't to mix."

"I wonder why," Preston said.

"Gee, I don't know. Papa's funny that way."

The bus settled into a long, straight pull down the road.

"Seems like a long way," Benjy said. "If we had a swimming pool at Mayville, we could go swimming every day."

"Yeah—and learn to do jackknife and everything!"

"I think we ought to get the fellows together and make a pool," Benjy declared. "We could dig the hole. I bet Murf Anderson would help. And maybe Joe, too."

"We might have a club and work on it together," Preston suggested. Then he turned to the window to watch the houses and fields go spinning by on the outside. He watched how the great bus did just what the driver wanted it to do. It must be fun to be a bus driver!

In almost no time they reached the city limits, and soon the bus pulled into the station.

Benjy knew exactly how to find the new swimming pool, and Preston enjoyed the walk through the city almost as much as the bus ride. He loved looking up at the high buildings with all their rows of windows, and he liked the roar of the city traffic. Cities were fun!

They recognized the big red building at once by the sign in front, which said "Swimming Pool—Grand Opening, Saturday, February 4. All boys and girls welcome." There was something else in small print below, but they didn't have time to read it.

Inside they found a noisy line of boys waiting to pass by the ticket booth window. Feeling suddenly a little shy, Preston dropped behind Benjy in the line. He grew more and more excited as they moved up closer to where he could hear the man at the window saying to each boy who went by, "Dressing rooms over to the left. Showers right behind. Thank you! Go right in, sonny!"

At last it was Benjy's turn. The man didn't even look at Benjy, but he said the same words again. "Fifteen cents, please. Dressing rooms to the left. Showers behind. Thank you, sonny. Have fun!"

Then Benjy was through the gate, and Preston, trembling a little, laid his dime and nickel on the window. The man reached out to sweep it into the pile of nickels and dimes on the other side of the bars.

"Fifteen cents, that's right," he began. Suddenly he stopped. He was looking at Preston! Preston thought his heart was going to stop beating.

"Oh—say—" the man said. Then he pushed the fifteen

cents back through the window. "Sorry. You come Monday night, son. Next boy!"

Just then Benjy turned and looked back.

"Hurry up, slow poke!" he called to Preston.

Preston swallowed, looked around, and suddenly realized that every other boy in the line was white!

"Move along, son!" the man repeated. "Monday night for colored."

"Take your money and move on, Bud," said the boy behind. "You're holding up the line."

Preston moved out of line and stood bewilderedly, trying to think what to do. He looked down at the bundle with the new red swimming trunks and the clean towel. He felt his lip quiver and bit it. He mustn't cry. He mustn't cry!

The doorway was jammed with people—strange and frightening people, all white. He had never felt so alone.

Then he heard Benjy's shrill voice.

"Where's my pal?" demanded Benjy of the ticket man.

"You mean the little colored boy?" the man asked. "He can't come in today."

"But the sign said *everybody*," Benjy said.

"Yep, but not on the same day, sonny," the man explained patiently. "You didn't read the fine print. It says colored on Monday night before the water's changed."

"I don't get it," Benjy persisted.

"Colored and white don't swim together—that's the rule. In or out now, and make it snappy!" said the man.

Benjy hesitated, then suddenly he pushed back through the gate and ducked behind the boy standing next in line.

"I already made up my mind!" he cried. "If my pal Pres can't go in, I won't either. You can keep your money and go jump in your old pool and—and drown for all I care!"

He pushed his way through the crowd, which opened to let him pass. "Come on, Pres!" he shouted, grabbing Preston's hand. "Let's go home. I don't think it's much of a place here anyhow."

The ride back to Mayville seemed to take a long, long time. Preston stared out of the window, although he didn't see anything. He couldn't even look at Benjy. Benjy suddenly was somebody else. Benjy could get in, and he couldn't! Benjy was white!

When at last they stopped on the Mayville corner and climbed off the bus (of course, it was just his luck), there were Murf Anderson and Joe Cotter, strolling down the street ahead of them.

"Hi ya, fellows!" Benjy shouted. Preston wished he'd shut up!

Joe and Murf stopped and waited. Joe looked neat and stuck-up as he always did, and Murf looked untidy, as he always did.

"Hey, Benjy!" Preston whispered. "Let's not stop."

"Where you guys been on the bus?" Murf asked.

"Gee, guess what!" Benjy exclaimed. "We went to that new swimming pool at Metrop, and they wouldn't let Preston in!" He bobbed his head up and down emphatically. "So I just told them I wouldn't go either!"

Murf looked a little sorry, but Joe shrugged his shoulders.

"You didn't think they'd let colored and white in together, did you?" he asked. "How silly can you guys get?"

Benjy went on talking. Preston wished he'd stop.

"I told Pres we ought to have a pool of our own," he declared. "We could dig it ourselves! And Pres said we could have a club, maybe, and do it all together!"

Murf looked excited. "That's an idea!" he exclaimed. "Let's have a club and have our own pool!"

Even Joe looked interested.

"Where—where'd we dig it?" he asked.

"Pres's back yard would do," Benjy suggested. "How about it, Pres?"

"I'm going home," Preston said. "You can stay here."

He strode off. Joe and Murf dropped behind, but Benjy trotted right along, talking. Pres couldn't shake Benjy!

Mama was standing on the porch of the gray house, and (just his luck again) there was company. It was Mr. Huntington. Preston straightened his shoulders, trying to act as if nothing had happened at all. He paused under the crab apple tree and said in a loud voice, trying to sound casual, "Don't see any apples around any place!"

"Silly, it's February!" Benjy reminded him. "Hi!" he called to the folks on the porch. "We're back!"

Mama looked at Preston, and she *knew!* But she didn't

ask any questions. She just took the little bundle from him
—the red trunks that weren't even wet, and the towel.

"Look, honey, we've got company!" she said gaily.

"Hello!" said Mr. Huntington. He knew, too! Preston
could tell.

"They wouldn't let Pres in till Monday night!" Benjy
exclaimed. "And I wouldn't go either. Wasn't that a gyp?"

Before Mr. Huntington could answer, Mama said quickly, "Guess what! We've just heard there's going to be a
new family moving in across the street!"

"There's a boy about your age, I think," Mr. Huntington
added. "They're Italians."

"Gee-oh, dagos!" cried Benjy. "That'll finish Papa!
We'll sure have to move now. He says first it was nig—" he
stopped and blushed.

"Come on, fellow!" Mr. Huntington said to Benjy.
"We'd better let these folks have some lunch. Good-by,
Mrs. Harlow. Good-by, Preston." Gently he pushed Benjy
down the walk.

Preston barely heard him. He hurried into the house.
Mama came in quietly, shutting the door. She didn't even
look at him.

"Preston!" she called crossly. Mama was almost never
cross. "Preston, don't you ever let me hear you calling that
new boy a dago, hear?"

Preston didn't answer. He didn't have to. Mama had
said just the right thing!

CHAPTER 2 NEW NEIGHBORS

Mr. Huntington's announcement about the new family was followed up the very next day by the exciting arrival of the Lubranos, with the shabbiest moving van Preston and Benjy had ever laid eyes on. When a year before, the Andersons had come up from the South, they'd brought very little besides themselves.

"But eleven children is plenty!" Benjy's father had exclaimed.

The Lubranos, as Mr. Weinberg put it, brought everything with them except the Bay of Naples. "I wonder if they left anything in Italy at all!" he sighed. "They sure brought all the ancient ruins!" When Benjy told him they'd come from Metropolis, not Italy, he just shook his head.

It took half a day for the unloading, what with stoves and tables and chairs and carpets and boxes of dishes. From early morning until late afternoon two husky movers hauled furniture off the van and in through the front door. Rumor said that Mr. Lubrano was planning to open a little fruit store right there in the living room, which troubled the neighbors. Mrs. Harlow thought it would be handy to have a fruit store so close, but Mr. Weinberg was appalled. He couldn't think which was worse—the fruit store in the front room or the household clutter on the street. "Trash—all trash!" he mourned.

There really was a great deal of debris. Paper and boxes lay everywhere. Some of the dishes in the boxes had been broken and were tossed out on the sidewalk. Even the Andersons looked at the disorder with quiet amazement.

It was hard luck that there had to be school on moving day, because the ones who could most enjoy the excitement were imprisoned until most of it was over. But directly after school all the children in the block, among them Preston and Benjy and Joe and all eleven of the Andersons, raced back to Fourth Place to watch. A little farther away, and less conspicuously, the older folk were watching, too. Mr. and Mrs. Weinberg stood in their front yard, shaking their heads. Mrs. Anderson stood out on her front porch, and Mrs. Harlow watched from a living room window. Earlier in the afternoon she had taken over some coffee and cookies, but the gesture had not been well received.

"They said they like it stronger!" she said to Preston, when he came in once for a drink of water.

"They" as far as Preston and Benjy could see, were a short man, a large woman, and a thin, little, dark-eyed boy with long hair that hung over his face untidily. The man, who must be Mr. Lubrano, kept shouting in Italian to the woman, who stood by the door looking worried and frightened. The boy pretended not to see anybody.

"Looks like they didn't want to come here much," Benjy observed. "But that's nothing to how we don't want them to come!"

The Lubranos certainly didn't like the audience of children, and very soon all three of the family retired behind the house, leaving the movers with the unloading job. Someone—perhaps it was Murf Anderson—began to clap. The other children clapped and cheered. And the next thing to happen was that a big piece of broken crockery hurtled through the air, landing at Benjy's feet. Benjy quickly leaned over, picked up the piece, and hurled it back. It crashed against the side of the house, and there followed from the back yard a storm of small stones. The children dashed off in every direction. Benjy and Preston escaped to the Weinberg's front yard.

"Gee, it must have been that boy!" Benjy exclaimed. "You wouldn't think anybody so little could throw so fast!"

The last stone hit Mr. Weinberg's shoulder, and when he jumped, his glasses fell off. Luckily they landed in the dry grass. He picked them up and looked them over tenderly to be sure there were no chips or cracks. Then he shook his fist as he retreated to the porch steps where Mrs. Weinberg stood wringing her hands.

"Baah!" shouted Mr. Weinberg. "They cost thirty dollars! What a neighborhood! First it's niggers, then it's poor white trash. Now it's dagos. And what next, I ask you!"

He seemed to be asking Preston, and perhaps because he was still wiping his glasses, he didn't see Preston stiffen. But Benjy did.

"Papa!" cried Benjy in distress. "Papa!"

"Come inside!" commanded Mr. Weinberg. "Both of you come inside this house. Look as if they didn't be there!" Mr. Weinberg was likely to speak in the Yiddish way when excited. "Come in, Benjy. Come inside, Preston. This rough stuff respectable people will not permit."

Preston shook his head. Mr. Weinberg looked annoyed and pushed him toward the house.

"Papa!" cried Mrs. Weinberg. "Look what you said!"

Taking Preston's hand, she said comfortingly, "Come inside, little one. Papa didn't mean not one word of it!"

Mr. Weinberg was bewildered.

"What did I say?" he demanded, puzzled.

"Papa, you called Preston a nigger!" Benjy cried.

"But I never! Preston is a good boy!" exclaimed Mr. Weinberg. "Come back here, Preston!"

Preston had started for the sidewalk, and stopped unwillingly. He knew Mr. Weinberg hadn't meant anything—but—a stone hit the walk at his feet, and he came back.

"I apologize, Preston!" Mr. Weinberg exclaimed, leading him inside the house and pushing him into a large upholstered chair. "It was I spoke in haste. It was because of the dagos! I wouldn't hurt your feelings!"

"And we will have some of the bagels!" Mrs. Weinberg said warmly, as she hurried out toward the kitchen. Mrs. Weinberg was fat, and Preston noticed how the lamp shades jiggled when she hurried. She was nice! "And a taste of the good blackberry juice, yes?" she coaxed, as she passed Preston a plate of the crunchy bagels.

"Come on, Pres!" Benjy urged him. "Papa got excited. He wasn't even thinking about you, Pres!"

"Of course not!" Mrs. Weinberg said earnestly. "Preston is a good boy!"

Preston sat upright in the big chair. He still felt nervous.

"All such a fuss over a lot of dagos!" Mr. Weinberg muttered.

"Papa!" pleaded Benjy. "It made Pres think of the swimming pool when you said that. You know about it?"

Mr. Weinberg didn't know, and while Preston sat silently, crunching his bagel, Benjy poured out the story.

"I just told them if my pal Pres couldn't go swimming, I wouldn't either. I did! Wasn't that right, Papa?"

Mr. Weinberg bristled with indignation.

"You did exactly right, my boy!" he cried. "I'm proud of you. They ought to be glad to have Preston swim there! And with his new red trunks! I'm proud of you!"

He thumped his fingers on the chair. Then his face clouded again as he thought of the new neighbors.

"Eyetalians! Spoiling our nice neighborhood. Throwing around crockery and stones. Smelling like spaghetti. Paah!" He looked as if he were smelling the spaghetti right then.

It was all so pleasant, with Mrs. Weinberg cooing softly and the curtain fringes swinging cheerfully that Preston almost forgot the new neighbors.

Suddenly the cuckoo clock began to buzz. The little bird, which always fascinated Preston, leaped out and chimed— one, two, three, four, five.

"Gee!" Preston exclaimed. "It's five. I've got to go."

He walked to the door and looked down the street.

"Everything's quiet!" he said.

"You come back, Preston!" Mrs. Weinberg said warmly. "You come back every day!"

"I'll walk you home," Benjy offered.

The van was gone. The Lubranos seemed to be settled somewhere back in the big house. Nothing remained of the afternoon affair except the debris on the sidewalk. The boys stepped over the pieces gingerly.

"Murf Anderson's folks never had anything as bad as this!" Benjy chuckled. "Pres, you aren't mad at Papa, are you?"

"Gee, no!" Preston said heartily. "I like your papa and your mama, too. They're nice."

"I guess Papa means it about moving," Benjy said.

"I wish you didn't have to go," Preston sighed.

"Yeah! But you know how he is when he gets his head set."

Just then a thought struck Preston. "Say!" He almost stumbled over a broken chair rocker, kicked it aside, and looked to see if anyone was coming. All was quiet.

"Say what?" asked Benjy.

"I got an idea! What about getting the guys together to— to clean this stuff up? Maybe that would please your papa."

"But those dagos wouldn't let us do it, Pres!"

"But if we could get that kid—in with us—"

Benjy was doubtful.

"He'd break up our crowd. Anyway, he wouldn't do it, I bet. I bet he's a bad 'un."

"It—it wouldn't hurt to try."

"Well, O.K., if you want to," Benjy agreed at last.

Preston puckered up his lips and whistled softly.

No answer from the Lubrano house! He whistled again.

Two black eyes and part of a tousled black head appeared, peeking around the back corner of the house. The boys could barely see them through the shadows.

"Hi!" Preston called in the friendliest tone he could make. Benjy echoed a weak "Hi!" and both stood ready to run if another rock should come round the corner. Nothing came, but there was still no answer. The black eyes stared.

"Hey, do you want to be in our club?" Preston said, still trying to sound friendly.

The boy came out from his hiding place. He was small and thin, but he looked about their age, Preston thought.

"What club?" the boy asked suspiciously.

"Come on out and we'll tell you," Preston invited him. The boy ventured a little closer.

"You better not throw at me!" he muttered.

"We won't. It's the club on this block," Preston assured him. "We have fun, and you can belong if you want to."

"Well—" There was a stirring sound from behind the house. Something banged, and a strident voice called.

"Angelo! You come back here. You get inside!" Some Italian words followed. The boy answered in Italian and scampered. There was mumbling and then silence.

Preston and Benjy waited a moment and then went on.

"I guess that's that!" Benjy said. "I told you so."

"Guess you're right," Preston admitted.

"Funny, wasn't it? They threw at us, and then we threw back at them," Benjy observed.

"Maybe they got scared with so many people watching."

"Well—" Benjy whistled a little tune. "I better go home. See you." He turned away, still whistling.

That instant, in the darkness, they heard another whistle. Through the shadows somebody was coming stealthily. When he came up closer, they saw that it was the Lubrano boy.

"Hey!" he called softly.

"Hey yourself," Preston said quickly.

The boy stood awkwardly on the walk. They could see that his clothes were shabby, and he looked cold, too.

"Why don't you come to my house?" Preston said.

"Don't want to," the boy answered.

"Well, don't then," Benjy said tartly.

"Better come," Preston urged. "You had a big day."

"Yeah." The boy was silent again. Then suddenly he spoke. "I'll join your club if you want me to," he said.

"O.K.!"

"Don't you tell my pop."

"We're not going to," Benjy said, still annoyed.

"What does the club do?"

"Oh, we just get together and have fun," Preston said.

"We're going to make a swimming pool," added Benjy.

"We might have a meeting—maybe Saturday!" Preston said, thinking fast. No time to lose if they wanted the Italian kid in with them.

"Where at?"

Preston and Benjy looked at each other. Things were moving a little faster than they had planned.

"Well—" Preston had another inspiration. "We—we might meet in the basement of Central Church. People are always meeting there for things," he explained. "I bet Mr. Huntington would let us."

The Italian boy stiffened. "In your church? That's a sin!"

"A—a what?"

"We're Catholics," the boy explained.

"What's that got to do with it?" Benjy demanded. "I'm a Jew, and I guess it's all right for me!"

"Well—if it's down in the basement, I might," Angelo said hesitantly. "But don't you tell my pop."

"I said we wouldn't," Benjy retorted. "But why not?"

"He don't like niggers and kikes, that's why." Then he amended, "My mother wouldn't care, but she—she's sick."

Benjy bristled. Then he laughed.

"My dad doesn't like dagos!" he said.

The boy cringed, and Preston felt sorry for him.

"What's your name?" he asked.

"Angelo. Angelo Lubrano."

Preston told Angelo his name and Benjy's.

"Have you got any brothers and sisters?" he asked Angelo.

"Yeah," Angelo said. "I got two little sisters, but they stay with my aunt in Metropolis 'cause my mother's sick."

"Too bad," Benjy said. "What's the matter with her?"

"I—I don't know exactly." Angelo's voice trembled. "She—she might have to have an operation!"

Preston and Benjy were a little embarrassed. For a minute they didn't say anything.

"Well, I got to git!" Angelo said. "If my pop was to know I was here, he'd kill me!" He was gone in the shadows almost before he'd stopped talking.

Preston and Benjy looked at each other.

"Whew!" Benjy whistled. "How do you like that! So

they don't like niggers and kikes. Who do they think they are anyway!"

"He acted like he was scared about his mother," Preston said.

"Yeah. That's tough! Gee! What if she'd die!" Benjy exclaimed.

Preston felt a lump in his throat. He'd been so small when his father had died that he couldn't remember a great deal, but he recalled how lonely and sad they'd been and how worried Mama had felt when she had to take a job that kept her from Pearl and himself for part of the day.

"I—I wonder what's so special about being a Catholic," he said finally.

"Oh, they're funny," Benjy said. "Do you think the fellows will like Angelo?"

"I wonder if Joe Cotter will."

"Well—" Benjy hesitated. "You can't always tell. Joe's stuck-up, but every now and then he surprises you. Murf Anderson ought to like him all right, I guess. Anyway, the club is started!"

"We've got to have that meeting now, sure enough!"

"Yeah, no backing down. You sure did some quick talking there! Well, got to go. See you tomorrow." Benjy went off whistling.

The next day there was a "For Sale" sign posted on the Weinberg house.

CHAPTER 3   JUST ANYBODY CAN'T
BE PRESIDENT

The excitement over the Lubranos and the plans for the club made Preston almost forget about his disappointment at Metropolis. With so much going on, a fellow couldn't worry about something that was all over and done with!

There was a lot of work to be done. To begin with, the meeting had to be planned. Mr. Huntington said he'd be pleased to have the boys come to the church basement on Saturday morning. He even promised to drop in himself to see how things were going. Murf Anderson was sold on the swimming pool idea and promised that his twin brothers Peter and Paul would join in the digging. Joe Cotter was interested. He wasn't so sure he wanted to be tied up with the neighborhood club, but he agreed to be around on Saturday morning to see what was up. And Angelo said he'd try to come if they were sure that they would meet in the basement.

Friday night Preston had strange dreams—all about swimming and Mr. Weinberg shouting, "We won't move away." He remembered to tell that part of the dream to Benjy on their way to the church the next morning. Benjy hoped it meant good luck.

In spite of his bold words to Angelo, Benjy was a little nervous because this was the first time he had been in a church. He didn't like the dim basement room either.

"Mighty dark down here!" he remarked. "Reckon they'll ever find the place?"

"Murf will," Preston said. "And Joe, too—if he comes."

"I don't care if Joe comes or not," Benjy said. "I don't like that guy!"

Preston said he didn't either. "But my mother says you usually like people when you know them," he added.

"I don't want to know him any better," Benjy said.

But Joe came and so did Murf. Peter and Paul were busy helping their father with a paint job, but Murf promised they'd be on hand to "dig" when the time came.

"Mighty small club!" Joe remarked. "Is the new kid coming?"

"You mean the dago?" Murf asked.

"He said he might," Preston said. "Maybe that's him now."

Joe jumped up to answer the rap on the door. Sure

enough, it was Angelo. He looked frightened and as if he weren't sure he belonged here at all.

"Well, come on in," Joe said. "Don't keep holding the door open. This is the place!"

Angelo sidled in hesitantly. Preston smiled at him, but Angelo looked away from Preston and followed Joe to the other side of the table.

"Hey, Angelo, what you scared of?" Benjy asked him.

Angelo's black eyes snapped.

"I'm not scared!" he exclaimed, and moved closer to Joe. It made Preston a little sore. After all, he thought, he and Benjy had been the ones to invite him. Anybody would have thought he was Joe's special friend. And then Preston noticed an odd thing. Joe actually seemed to like the Italian boy!

"Look here, fellows," Joe said, speaking especially to Benjy. "This kid's new, and it's against his religion to be in this church. You'd be scared, too."

"It's against my religion, too!" said Benjy. "What about that?"

"Oh, well," Joe said. "Jews are different."

"Everybody's different!" Preston exclaimed. "But everybody's the same, too!" It was a new idea!

"That's right!" Benjy took it up. "We're even different colors. Pres's real dark brown, and Angelo kind of brown, and Joe and Murf are real white, and—"

"You're sort of in between!" Murf exclaimed. "And

there's some people that are red, too—they're Indians. We got lots of Indians in the South."

"Is that so?" Benjy was interested. "What makes them red. Is their blood the same color as ours?"

"I guess so," Murf said. "Blood's the same with everybody, don't you s'pose? What color's yours, Pres?"

Preston said it was red. They were all so interested that they didn't notice when Mr. Huntington came into the room.

"Hello, there!" he said. "How are things going?"

"Well—" Preston was a little embarrassed. "We haven't got started yet. We—we've just been talking."

"I think we ought to get down to business," Murf remarked. "You'll stay, won't you, Mr. Huntington?"

"Sure you want an old man here?" the minister asked.

"You're not old!" exclaimed Benjy.

"Thanks!" Mr. Huntington laughed. "I'll sit in for a while. Carry on."

"Well—" Preston began. "I guess we ought to talk about what this club is going to do."

"We're going to build a swimming pool, aren't we?" Murf asked. "That's what I came for anyhow."

"Won't it take a lot of money?" Joe asked.

"Not if we dig it ourselves, it won't."

The other boys looked at Mr. Huntington.

"I'm afraid you've picked a pretty big project," he admitted. "There's a good deal more than digging to it. And of course you've got to have a place to dig. Frankly, it'll cost money—I don't know how much."

"Well—" Preston felt a little dashed. "What do you fellows think?"

They all looked serious and concerned. Suddenly it seemed as if they wanted that pool more than anything in the world.

Finally Benjy spoke. "I think we can do it!" he declared. "Maybe it'll take a long time. But we can get the money for it!"

"Why don't we put it up to the church and have them take a collection?" Joe asked. "The church has got more money than we have."

"But we're the ones that want the swimming pool!" Preston exclaimed. "It was our idea!"

"Well—maybe you're right at that," Joe admitted. "But if some of them heard about it and offered to help, it would be all right for us to take the money, wouldn't it?"

Mr. Huntington laughed.

"I think it would be a shame to deny them the pleasure. But I think with Preston that it's your idea, and you'd better start the ball rolling yourselves."

"I could get a job," Murf suggested. "They need a new carrier on the Mayville Bugle."

"I can run errands for the stores in town," Benjy said. "They'll give me tips. And Angelo, couldn't you get tips for deliveries from your father's store?"

"Well—" Angelo hesitated. "I could get some, but not much. My mother has to have an operation and—"

Joe exclaimed suddenly, "Benj, you stop nagging at this kid, hear?"

"O.K., smart guy, so how are you going to pay?" Benjy demanded. "Or will your mother let you be in the club?"

It looked as if trouble were brewing, and Mr. Huntington said hastily, "Say, kids, I'm one of the church folks you've sold your pool idea to, so here's my contribution to start things off." He laid a dollar bill on the table in front of them.

"The first dollar for the swimming pool!" Preston exclaimed. "Gee, thanks!"

"Mr. Huntington, you're a right guy!" Benjy exclaimed. "I got some money, too. Here it is." He jingled some coins in his pocket and put several dimes and nickels on top of the dollar bill. Murf had a little money, and Preston, remembering the fifteen cents for swimming that he hadn't used, dug it out of his wallet.

"It grows pretty fast," Murf said.

"Yeah!" Benjy sighed. "We'll just about get the swimming pool, and then I'll have to move!"

"Maybe we can do something about that!" exclaimed Mr. Huntington. "You talk it over and let me know. I'm back of you, but I've got to leave now."

From the door he saluted, and they all chorused, " 'Bye now!"

"Hey, Benj," Murf said then, "what's the big idea—that sign in your yard?"

"Well, my father says things aren't like they used to be," Benjy explained. "He says the neighborhood's getting run-down, and we'll have to move."

"What does he mean by 'run-down'?" Murf demanded.

"I know," Joe said. "My mother says the same thing."

"Everybody moves out, and new ones move in," Benjy continued. "There's so many—strangers."

"Mama says strangers aren't strangers after you get to know them," Preston commented. "Mr. Huntington says so, too."

"But things don't *look* the same," Joe insisted. "Things on the street aren't kept up any more!"

"I guess it's our empty lot," Benjy said. "Papa said he wasn't going to have it cleaned off when everybody kept dumping trash there."

"Yeah, it's partly our fault," Preston admitted. "You can't blame Mr. Weinberg."

"And there's junk on the sidewalks and other places," Benjy suggested, looking up at the ceiling. "My father says property is going down."

"What does that mean?" asked Murf.

"It means you don't get as much money when you sell your house," Joe explained. "And my mother says there's liable to be de-delinquency."

"What's that?" Murf asked again.

Nobody knew exactly, but Preston had an idea and tried to explain.

"It's what you do when you haven't got anything to do," he said. "You get to making a racket, and people get mad at you."

"Like the coke disappearing over at the schoolhouse," Joe said. "*Somebody* stole it!"

"I didn't!" shouted Murf.

"Nobody said you did!" Joe said quickly. "But whoever did—that's delinquency!"

"Yeah, and when you go home after school and haven't got anything to do except listen to the radio, and you try to find something interesting to do. That's what the grownups are always talking about."

"Well, they won't need to worry about us any more!" Murf exclaimed. "Not if we all go to work!"

The boys laughed. But Preston felt there was something else he wanted to say.

"I wish—I wish—" he began, and stopped.

"I wish my pop didn't want to move!" Benjy said.

"That's it!" Preston said. "If—if the street was clean, and if the weeds were cut and everything—"

"Yeah—and some of the houses could stand painting," Murf said. "My pop's a painter, and he thinks they all need a coat!"

"Why don't you paint your own house then?" Joe asked quickly.

Murf stared at him. "We never even thought about it!" he exclaimed. "It's not our house."

"And then"—Benjy looked at Angelo hesitatingly—"maybe you—we could pick up some of that stuff from the moving. With your mother sick and your dad starting the store, I guess you need help."

Angelo flushed. "What does it matter about the outside?" he asked. "You ought to see how nice it is inside, where we live!"

They all laughed.

"All Mr. Weinberg can see is the outside," Joe explained gently. "Nobody knows what it's like inside, and they get the wrong idea."

"Well—" Angelo still looked puzzled.

"Let's start on the empty lot first," Preston suggested. "We could do that next Saturday, if it doesn't rain."

"O.K.," Murf said. "That's what this club is going to do then. One—clean up the block, and two—get the swimming pool. Say, what's the name of the outfit anyway?"

"Is Fourth Place Club all right?" Benjy asked.

"Sure!" the others agreed.

"What about girls?" Joe asked. "I'm afraid my sister will want to join."

"No girls, or you can count me out," Murf exclaimed. "We got so many girls at our house, that if they all joined the club, it would be a girls' club!"

"No girls," Preston agreed, but he felt a little sorry on

his sister Pearl's account. "Anyway, they wouldn't want to work on the lot," he added.

"They can swim in the pool," suggested Benjy, magnanimously.

"We ought to have a president," Murf said.

"Preston's the one to be president," said Benjy. "The club was his idea."

"No, he can't!" exclaimed Joe. "Pres couldn't be president of a white club. He'd have to be president of a Negro club."

"I don't see why," Benjy said stubbornly.

"I don't know, but that's the way it is," Joe insisted. "Same way that you'd have to be president of a Jew club. See?"

Preston didn't look at anyone. It wasn't that he wanted to be president, he told himself. But—

"Does there have to be a president?" Angelo asked suddenly in a small voice. They all gave a start. Joe laughed and clapped him on the back.

"Good idea, kid!" he exclaimed. "We don't need any officers!"

"Except somebody to take care of all our money," Murf reminded them.

"I reckon Pres can do that all right, can't he?" Benjy asked. "He can be treasurer."

"Oh, sure, that's O.K.," Joe agreed. "I never heard anything against it. It's just presidents that count."

"All right, then," Benjy said quickly, and shoved the little heap of money across the table to Preston.

"You better put it in the bank, Pres," he said. "We ought to have a bank account."

Preston felt better about the president business now. Being treasurer sounded exciting.

"All right," he said, putting the money into his wallet. "I'll take it to the bank Monday."

"How much is there?" Joe asked. "Anybody count it?"

Nobody had, so Preston poured it all out on the table again. There were three dollars and twenty cents.

"Not bad!" Murf whistled. "We'll get that pool yet. I'll go to the Bugle office right now. They're open till noon."

Angelo had to hurry back to the fruit store, and he and Joe went out together. Benjy and Preston were left.

"Look's like Joe's found a buddy!" Benjy commented. "Funny, isn't it? You and I were the ones that got Angelo to come, but he'll hardly talk to us!"

"I guess it's on account of his father," Preston said. "But it's funny about Joe. Why do you suppose he likes Angelo?"

"Well, I'm glad he likes somebody," Benjy said. "What are you going to do with the money until the bank opens? How about the crab apple tree?"

Preston remembered the tin can in the niche between the tree roots where he and Benjy hid their treasures.

"Good idea! Reckon the old can's still there?"

"Reckon it's still got the false bottom I fixed in it?" Benjy added.

They hurried back toward Preston's house. The crab apple tree looked well able to protect the treasure (real treasure this time) and keep their secret.

Preston stooped down to brush some dry leaves out of the opening, and then dug farther into the niche at the tree's roots. There it was—the same old can! He poked around inside it and at last pulled out the round piece of tin —the false bottom!

While Benjy stood guard to see that no one was spying on their secret, Preston took the can, a little rusty now, tucked the bill and change carefully inside, and then pressed the piece of tin down over them. To make doubly sure, he filled the can to the top with dirt and leaves.

"Now bury it in there good!" Benjy cautioned.

Preston tucked it far back among the roots, out of sight. And then he put some leaves on top. At last he stood up and gazed critically at the hiding place.

"Does it look O.K.?" he asked Benjy.

"Should we tell the others?" Preston asked.

Benjy hesitated. "Oh, I guess so," he said finally. "It belongs to all of us. But nobody except our club ought to know!"

"Nobody but us!" Preston echoed, as he started on into his house and Benjy turned toward the gate.

The swimming pool was on its way!

Monday noon Preston ran all the way home from school, gobbled his lunch, and then jumped up from the table.

"Big business, I guess!" Mama exclaimed.

"Yes'm. This is banking day!" he told her.

She laughed and didn't ask any questions. That was Mama for you! Preston ran out to the tree, pushed away the leaves, and drew out the precious can. All safe! He thrust the money into his wallet. And now for the bank! Ten minutes if he ran!

He had never been in the bank alone, and suddenly it looked a great deal bigger than he had ever noticed. When he went up to the teller's window, the man on the other side was busy and didn't notice him at all. He waited and waited, but the man kept on writing figures on paper.

Finally, Preston went timidly over to the enclosure in front, where he could see Mr. Spriggs, the bank president, talking to a man who sat in the big green leather chair. Preston had seen Mr. Spriggs in church. He wondered if he dared walk in there and announce his presence. After a long time, the man got up to leave. And at last Mr. Spriggs looked over and saw him.

"Why, hello there, Preston!" he called. Mr. Spriggs knew him! "What can we do for you today?"

Preston said hesitatingly, "I—I want to put some money in the bank."

"Well, that's just what we like to have people do," Mr. Spriggs told him. "Suppose you come in here and do your business with me!"

So there was Preston, walking right through the little gate and sitting down in the big leather chair by the desk marked "President"!

"So you want to start an account!" Mr. Spriggs said kindly. "That's fine!" He got out a little black book and held his pen ready to write. "Preston Harlow—right?"

"It's for our club," Preston explained. "We started a club with Benjy Weinberg and Murf Anderson and Joe Cotter and Angelo Lubrano, and I'm the treasurer!"

"A club! Now what do you think of that!" Mr. Spriggs exclaimed. "What's the name of your club?"

Preston told him, and Mr. Spriggs wrote it in the book with his ball-point pen.

"Fourth Place Club. How much money do you want to deposit today, Mr. Treasurer?"

Preston handed him the three dollars and twenty cents.

"What are you going to do with all this money?" Mr. Spriggs asked, writing away in a little book.

Preston found himself telling all about how they had decided to clean up the neighborhood so Mr. Weinberg wouldn't move, and how they were going to raise money for a swimming pool.

When he finished, Mr. Spriggs showed him the amount written in the book.

"Looks pretty good!" he exclaimed. "But it would look better with one more dollar, I think." Just below the three dollars and twenty cents he wrote down one dollar.

"A swimming pool! A swimming pool!" he kept saying.

"It'll take a long time I guess," Preston admitted.

"Sure will! But you can do it. It's a fine idea," Mr. Spriggs said heartily, handing the book to Preston. He stood up then, and Preston did, too, knowing it was time to go. Mr. Spriggs was a busy man.

"By the way, have you got a job for yourself, son?" he asked then, instead of saying good-by.

Preston said he hadn't got one but was watching the ads.

"Can you do garden work?"

Preston certainly could.

"Well, then you go over and have a talk with my wife. Do you know where I live, Preston?"

Did Preston know? Indeed he did! Everybody in town knew where the great brick Spriggs house was!

"All right then. She wants a boy to work in her garden this spring. You tell her I sent you over there!"

Preston could hardly say thank you, as Mama had taught him to do, he was so excited. He could hardly get out of the bank. But he did overhear something Mr. Spriggs said to the clerk at the window. "The little colored boy wants to build a pool to swim in. Poor tyke!"

At other times that might have bothered him. But just now Preston was too busy thinking of more important things. He might even have a job. He might!

All afternoon he dreamed over his books in school, and without even waiting to tell Benjy any more than the barest details, he was off promptly at three to Mrs. Spriggs's house. At first he flew. Then he stopped running and walked. When he finally reached the long front walk, he went so slowly that it seemed miles to the big front door. Preston had never applied for a job before. And he wasn't sure he'd like Mrs. Spriggs. She came to church, but she didn't stand and talk on the way out. Everybody knew the Spriggses were rich. Some of the people wondered why they kept on coming to Central Church when so many were changing to the new church on the hill or going to Metropolis.

And the Spriggs house! It had never looked so big and imposing, with its high white front door. Preston drew a long breath and rang the doorbell.

The woman who came to the door wasn't Mrs. Spriggs. She was a Negro, like himself, and she wore a white cap and apron. She looked surprised to see him.

"I want to see Mrs. Spriggs, if you please," he said. "Mr. Spriggs told me to come."

"Oh," the woman hesitated, but just then Mrs. Spriggs herself came down the stairs looking very pretty.

"What is it, Harriet?" she asked. Then she saw Preston.

"Oh, hello there," she said to Preston, and he answered stiffly, "How do you do?"

"He says Mr. Spriggs sent him," Harriet explained.

"Why, yes, Harriet!" Mrs. Spriggs said. "This boy goes to our church. Come right in—let's see—this is Preston, isn't it?"

Preston nodded. "Mr. Spriggs said maybe you would want to have a—a gardener!" he explained.

Mrs. Spriggs looked a little surprised but invited him into the living room. It was the grandest room Preston had ever seen, and he sat a little gingerly on the edge of his gold tapestried chair. It was a beautiful chair but not as comfortable as the ones at home.

"But—but you're pretty small to be a gardener!" Mrs. Spriggs went on then, smiling at him. "You say my husband sent you?"

"Yes, ma'am. At the bank. I was there and he told me."

"You—you were in the bank?"

"Yes'm. I was putting in the money for our club."

"Your club? What club is that?"

"It just started," he explained. "It—it's for com—community betterment!" He remembered those words from church!

"That's wonderful!" she exclaimed. "Tell me about it."

It was a little harder to explain to Mrs. Spriggs than to Mr. Spriggs, but he told her about the club, and how they were planning to fix up Fourth Place so Mr. Weinberg wouldn't move.

"Who belongs to your club?" she asked with interest.

"Benjy Weinberg is one."

"Oh, yes, the little Jewish boy. He'll be a good member!"

"Yes'm. And Joe Cotter and Murf Anderson."

"Joe Cotter and—they're all white boys, aren't they?"

Preston had a strange feeling, like the one he had had at the swimming pool. But she went on quickly.

"It's a good idea to fix up Fourth Place. It does look bad. What else are you planning to do?"

He hesitated.

"We're going to build a swimming pool," he said finally. "That's what I wanted to get a job for—so I could put some money in for the swimming pool."

"A swimming pool?" Mrs. Spriggs looked amazed.

Preston nodded.

"You and Joseph Cotter and—" she repeated slowly. "Does Mrs. Cotter know about the club?"

Preston didn't know. He guessed so. "We have meetings in the church basement," he added.

"Then Mr. Huntington knows about the club?"

"Oh, yes," Preston said. "He helped us to start it. And Mr. Spriggs knows, too."

"Look, Preston," she said, suddenly getting up from her chair, "I want to make a phone call. Will you wait here for a minute or two? It won't take long."

She went out, closing the door behind her. Preston, sitting on the edge of the chair, waited nervously. He heard her calling a number and then saying hello to somebody, but he couldn't hear what she said.

A moment later the maid Harriet opened the door and went through the living room with a vase of flowers. She smiled at Preston. But she left the door open behind her so that Preston couldn't help hearing what Mrs. Spriggs was saying on the phone.

"We must have someone around here who can be trusted," she was saying. "Yes, I know the family. I know she's highly thought of in the neighborhood. And he is a nice child! But—for one thing, he's—he's awfully small!" She paused for a moment, listening, and then went on. "Well—but there's another thing. This—this club, for all of them, and swimming—somehow, I just can't quite feel right to encourage social integration of this kind. Yes, I know we've taken that view in the church. I know how the minister feels about it. But I still—"

Just then Harriet walked back across the room through the open door and shut it behind her, so that Preston couldn't hear any more. He didn't know the meaning of all the words he had heard. But they made him uneasy.

Presently Mrs. Spriggs came back into the room and sat down thoughtfully.

"Preston," she said—and her voice was ever so kind—"I— I want to think about this a little longer. You're a small boy, and there's a lot of heavy work for us to do here. I'm glad Mr. Spriggs sent you, and I'm glad you came. But suppose we wait for a few days before we decide. If you find something else you'd rather do in the meantime, I'll understand. I'd like to think it over. Is that all right?"

She looked so kind and concerned that Preston felt a little bit sorry for her.

"Sure!" he said warmly. "That's all right, Mrs. Spriggs. But I can do all kinds of work!"

She stood up then, and they walked over to the door. Mrs. Spriggs opened it for him and shook hands.

"Now you give my greetings to your mother, Preston," she said. "And tell your little sister hello. You'll hear from me. Just as soon as we can decide!"

"Sure," he said trying to sound cheerful. "Pearl's not my little sister, Mrs. Spriggs. She's older than I am."

She laughed. "Dear me!" she exclaimed. "You're so business-like that I thought you must be the head of the house!" She laughed again and reached over for a little box on top of the bookcase. "And—and you take this box of sweets home with you," she said.

He took it, but he didn't feel much interested in candy.

He kept on feeling worse as he went toward home. What had he done wrong? Was it really because he was too small that he didn't get the job?

Preston felt lonely. He felt small. He was glad to see the top of Mama's head through the high window. She was home from work.

"You're late, honey," she said, as he came in. "What happened?"

He told her about the bank. That was fun. Then he told her about Mrs. Spriggs and the job. And he gave her the candy. She put it on the table without opening it, and listened thoughtfully.

"Did I do right?" he asked her then. "What did she mean about 'social int—int—'?"

"You didn't do anything wrong," she assured him. "It would have been better to shut the door yourself and not listen. It's never a good idea to listen to what you're not meant to hear. But you didn't do wrong. And as for social integration"—Mama knew the word, all right—"that's something you'll know more about as time goes on. I wouldn't worry about it now."

"Was it like the Metropolis pool when Benjy and I couldn't go in?" he asked her.

"It was, and it wasn't," she said. "Mrs. Spriggs knows

you, and she likes you. She isn't used to thinking of Negro and white boys playing together, that's all."

"Is it wrong to play with white boys?" he asked.

"Some white people think so. And some Negro people think so, too," she said.

"What do you think?" he asked her. She laughed.

"I think you play with your friends, and I like it!" she said cheerfully. "I hope you'll always find the kind you can trust and be happy with. And I hope you'll always be a good friend yourself."

"And it doesn't matter about Negroes and whites?"

"It matters about *people*, Preston!" she said seriously. "You'll find good people and bad people, all colors. And you'll always have friends if you know how to be a good friend yourself."

"And it doesn't matter about color?" he asked again. It was so important to have it straight!

"It really doesn't matter!" she exclaimed, hugging him. "Of course, I prefer your color myself, but that's because you're mine, mostly!"

"And I like your color myself!" he repeated after her. They both laughed, and he felt good again. It didn't even matter about jobs.

"Let's have some candy, if it won't spoil your supper!" Mama suggested.

He really felt good! The candy tasted good, too. It was coconut.

CHAPTER 5 CLEAN UP DAY

By the time clean up day came around in mid-March, most of the neighborhood knew that Fourth Place was about to have its face lifted, and that the first step in the lifting process was to be the lot where they'd been dumping trash.

Mr. Weinberg was heartily in favor of the project. "And he ought to be," Mrs. Cotter commented. "The lot belongs to him!" Mrs. Harlow thought it was a good plan because the boys themselves had used the lot to play in for a long time. Mr. Huntington promised he'd be there to help. Mrs. Anderson was pleased because the lot was next door to her house, though she had to admit that the heaps of ashes had come mostly from the Anderson stoves. Some of the tin cans had come from their place, too.

Murf's new boss, Mr. Bigelow, who edited the Mayville

Bugle, put an item in the paper about it. The article gave the boys a thrill.

BIG PLANS AHEAD FOR FOURTH PLACE

We hear by the grapevine that one of the town's eyesores is on the way to becoming an eye opener. Several youthful citizens have undertaken the job of pulling weeds and shoveling tin cans. Let's give them a cheer! And let's all drive around to see what happens!

But in spite of the "cheer," when Saturday morning came, and Preston was ready to start out to the lot with his rake and his little wagon, he couldn't see a soul in sight. The block was empty, as if not a single boy lived there. It was chilly, too!

"Gee, looks like they'd come!" he exclaimed to Pearl, who was sweeping the sidewalk in front of the house. "After it was in the paper and everything!"

"Do you want me to come and help?" Pearl asked. She looked ready to drop her broom at once, but he quickly said, "No, thanks." Better not get any girls in on this right now!

Pearl looked disappointed, and Preston felt a little ashamed and lonely, too, as he trundled the wagon down the sidewalk toward the big empty lot. When he reached the corner on the other side of the Andersons' house, he stopped and tried to think what to do as a beginning.

It was the first time, he realized, that he'd ever looked

with both eyes at the lot. He couldn't remember when it hadn't looked as it did now, full of tall weeds and heaps of refuse. The only clear place was in the middle, where the boys often played ball. Preston wondered why he hadn't noticed how bad it all looked.

"We told Angelo they ought to pick up their moving stuff," he said to himself, "and we never thought about this mess!"

He looked critically over toward his own house. The crab apple tree was still bare, but it would soon be getting leaves. The front steps and the walk would be all right as soon as Pearl was through sweeping them. He turned back to the lot. My, but that lot was big!

Still nobody in sight! Preston jumped up and down a little to keep from getting cold.

A moment later he saw Angelo come out of the fruit shop with a big box on his thin shoulders. It looked as if he were going to be too busy to help. Well, Preston thought, Angelo wasn't big enough to be much help anyway.

Just then Benjy came hurrying out of his house and ran down to where Preston stood with the wagon.

"Hi, Pres!" he exclaimed. "Nobody else here?"

Preston shook his head. He was beginning to feel sorry for himself.

"Gee!" Benjy exclaimed. "I wish I didn't have to do errands first. I got to deliver nails and things. I said I'd be at the store at eight, and it's pretty nearly that now."

"Oh, well, I guess Murf and Joe will be along," Preston said.

"I'll come right after lunch," Benjy promised.

"O.K.! You're lucky to have a job!" Preston remarked drearily.

"Gee, you'll have one, too, I bet, before next Saturday! Oh, there come the fellows. Hi!" he called to Murf and Joe, who came out of their houses almost at the same instant.

Murf couldn't stay long, he said, because he had to get to the Bugle office to pick up the Saturday morning delivery. Joe hadn't a good excuse, but he frankly wasn't interested in cleaning up the lot.

"But what will people say?" Preston said. "It was in the paper that we'd do it. Besides, we said we would."

"*I* didn't make any promises," Joe insisted. "And my mother says she doesn't expect us to anyway. I guess nobody will be surprised."

"Well, I think we have to do it," Preston said firmly. "If you fellows don't want to help, you don't have to. Benjy and I will get it done." He picked up his rake angrily.

Joe gasped. "Well, keep your shirt on, Pres!" he said. "I didn't say I wouldn't help. I just reminded you I didn't make any promises. It was Murf who put that piece in the paper."

"I told Mr. Bigelow about it," Murf admitted. "But I'll be back this evening to help. I promise. 'Bye now!"

"What're we going to do with all the stuff?" Joe asked, after Murf had gone.

"Well, I guess we get all the trash together and then—"

"It will be an awful pile, if we get it together. It'll take more fellows working, Pres."

Preston agreed.

"And it will take something big to haul the stuff away after we get the place cleared and the weeds pulled. What we need is about ten people working, and—and—a truck!"

Just at that instant Preston had an idea—a great idea!

"Joe!" he exclaimed. "I'm thinking of something. I'm thinking of several things. But—would it be all right if some other people—the girls—came to help?"

"Oh, sure, if you could get them."

"Pearl would, I think—and the Anderson girls would if we—if we—"

Ideas kept coming so fast that Preston hadn't even time to explain them.

"Joe!" he exclaimed. "You get your sister Rosanne if you can, and tell Pearl I said to come on, and go over to the Andersons and tell them—tell them we're going to have a big party!"

Joe looked dumbfounded. "What do you mean—party?" he demanded.

"It's O.K. We'll do something. Anyway, get them. And I'll be back in a jiff. I got to go see Mr. Huntington."

Joe looked bewildered, but Preston couldn't stop to explain. He was on his way to the church office almost before the last words were out.

The office window was opened a little, showing that Mr. Huntington was there. Maybe this was going to be a lucky day after all! Preston knocked on the door.

"Hi!" Mr. Huntington greeted him. "How's the big project going over on the Place?"

"Well—not so fast right now," Preston admitted. "But I think it will be all right."

"Need some more recruits?" Mr. Huntington asked. "I'm pretty good at hard work myself."

Preston laughed.

"Yeah, we need somebody to help all right," he said. "But we need something else, too. Mr. Huntington, you know how we go on picnics in the summer?"

"Yes." Mr. Huntington was puzzled.

"In that big truck, I mean."

"That's right—we rent a pickup from Mr. Dudley at the brickyard."

"Yeah! That one! That's what we need right now. Could we rent a truck"—he blurted it out and added—"to carry stuff to the dump?"

Mr. Huntington gasped. "Well—" he said thoughtfully, "I think I see what you mean. But it's a little expensive. Do you think you could afford it?"

"We've got four dollars and twenty cents," Preston said.

"Oh!" That was all Mr. Huntington would say, but

Preston suspected it wasn't enough money. He waited anxiously.

"Tell you what!" Mr. Huntington said finally. "You go over to the brickyard and see what Mr. Dudley says. He's the manager, and he belongs to the church, so he'll make you a good rate. I'll give him a ring while you're on the way, and then you can see what he says."

The brickyard was at the far edge of town, but Preston was a fast walker. Mr. Dudley was expecting him, too.

Grumpily, he said, "So this is the Fourth Place Club, getting somebody to do its job, eh!"

Preston's heart fell. He couldn't tell whether Mr. Dudley was angry or just being natural. Preston tried to keep his tongue from getting dry.

"Yes, sir!" he said. "I mean no, sir—"

"Speak up. What *do* you mean?" Mr. Dudley barked.

"We—we got to take all that stuff to the dump!" Preston finally managed to get it out. "And my wagon is too little!"

"Your wagon? What kind of wagon have you got?" Mr. Dudley shouted. Then Preston noticed he had a hearing aid. That must be what made him yell so loud. He was deaf!

Preston stood up closer and shouted back.

"I got a little one that you pull by hand."

"No good!" growled Mr. Dudley.

"Y-yes, sir!"

"Now listen, sprout!" Mr. Dudley shouted. "If you fellows get that place cleaned up, we'll rent you the truck to pull it off to the city dump."

"Thank you—" Preston began, but Mr. Dudley wasn't through.

"Who do you think is going to drive it?" he demanded.

"I—I don't know!" Preston said.

"Well, sir, I'll tell you who!" Mr. Dudley roared, and at last Preston could tell he was in a good humor! "*I'm* going to drive the truck. I'm going to come around there at one o'clock sharp, and if I find that stuff ready, I'll haul it away."

"Thank you—" Preston began again. But Mr. Dudley had more to say.

"How much do you think this is going to cost you?"

"I—I don't know," Preston said weakly. "How much does it usually cost?"

"Sprout!" exclaimed Mr. Dudley. "The cost of a truck for service is ten dollars minimum!"

"But— but—" Preston could hardly speak. "We haven't got that much," he said finally.

"That's just the point," Mr. Dudley chuckled. "It's reduced for public service. This will cost you exactly four dollars!"

"That's what we've got!" Preston gasped.

Mr. Dudley chuckled again. "Now isn't that queer!" he exclaimed. "I can't understand it!"

Preston couldn't either, right then. But a moment later, racing back to the empty lot, he remembered how Mr. Huntington had picked up the phone just as he was leaving.

The town clock struck nine when he reached the lot.

Joe was there, and so was Angelo. But not a thing had been touched. They were tossing a ball back and forth— not working at all. Preston's heart sank. Joe hadn't so much as picked up a tin can. And he probably hadn't even tried to get the girls! But there was no time to fuss about it.

"Fellows," Preston cried breathlessly, "we got to get this stuff cleared up by one o'clock sharp! Now Joe, you go get the Andersons like I said, and I'll get Pearl."

"What's the rush?" Joe inquired.

"There's a truck coming at one!" Preston told him. Even Joe was impressed.

Suddenly everything began to move fast. Pearl was just finishing the dishes, but almost before Preston had told them what was happening Mama grabbed the towel and Pearl had her sweater on and was racing over to the Andersons'. Joe was already back at the lot with Rosanne, and Preston never knew when Murf and the twins arrived, he was so busy hunting up hoes and rakes and bushel baskets. Once when he looked around he noticed that Mr. Huntington was there busy at work. And Mr. Huntington raised both hands and shook them together, laughing.

The lot began to change magically. Preston never had seen things move so fast.

"This is worth singing over!" he heard Mr. Huntington shout, and then he began "Whistle While You Work!" and everybody joined in.

At noon—and nobody ever did realize it was noon— Mrs. Harlow appeared with sandwiches and cocoa for the whole crowd.

"No time to go home right now, I guess!" she exclaimed.

Mrs. Weinberg and Mrs. Anderson both came, too, because the excitement seemed to be catching. The real joke happened when Benjy and Mr. Weinberg got home for lunch at noon, with their work done, and found the house empty. Of course it didn't take long to discover the crowd on the lot, although as Mr. Weinberg said, by that time it looked like a foreign country. The lot had never looked this way!

"It *ist wunderbar,* wonderful!" he kept saying and rubbing his hands together happily.

"Such good children!" Mrs. Weinberg cooed.

The only parents who weren't there were Mr. and Mrs. Lubrano and Mrs. Cotter. Mrs. Cotter did walk by once, to be sure that Joe wasn't getting too tired. The Lubranos stayed inside. But they didn't call Angelo home.

And how Angelo worked!

"You sure pack a wallop!" Benjy praised him.

"I got some flower seeds, and I'm going to plant them around the edge when it's time!" Angelo beamed. "I'm good at flowers!"

"I heard Italians always are!" Preston said. Angelo grinned again. He seemed to have forgotten his fear.

One small thing worried Preston. He had made a promise—only a sort of promise, but it bothered him. He'd said there would be a party, and then all the girls had come, and the word must have gone round. He wondered if he should tell Mama and ask her about it.

Promptly at one o'clock the big truck from the brickyard pulled up by the lot.

"Public service!" Mr. Dudley shouted. "Get to work everybody! Pile all this stuff on the truck!"

Mr. Huntington led the job, and soon everyone was busy

working. It was wonderful to see Mr. Weinberg working away just like Benjy.

How Mr. Bigelow of the Bugle heard about it Preston wasn't sure. Murf must have told him. But just as the big truck was ready to go off with its load of refuse and children, there suddenly was a man from the newspaper with a big camera.

"You grownups get out of the way!" he commanded briskly. "This is the kids' day. Where are those Fourth Placers? Put the Fourth Place Club in front!"

And then he snapped his bulb!

Mr. Huntington remarked, as the motor was starting, that it was the first dumping party he'd ever been on, and that it ought to be a real one with refreshments. The first stop then, was the ice cream store, where everybody had a double decker ice cream cone, any flavor he wanted!

The empty lot was clean as a whistle! A dumping party with ice cream! Pictures in the paper! Surely nothing more could happen in one day, Preston thought. But the day wasn't over yet.

When he struggled home at last, and wearily climbed up the front steps, he heard Mama calling him.

"Well, slow poke," she laughed, as he opened the door, "can't you hurry a little faster to hear some news?"

"News?" He thought he'd had about all the excitement he could stand. But Pearl was dancing up and down.

"You got a phone call!" she burst out finally.

"A—a—"

"It was Mrs. Spriggs!" Pearl cried. "And she said to call back right away!"

His hands shook as he picked up the phone. When Mrs. Spriggs answered, she sounded so friendly!

"I'm glad you called, Preston!" she exclaimed. "Have you made any other plans about working?"

"N-no, ma'am," he said, trying to keep his voice steady.

"Well, I've just been over at the lot and seen what a big job you boys have done there. I hear that you did most of it."

"No, ma'am—all the kids—the girls—" he stammered, and she laughed. She sounded almost like Mama when she laughed!

"Well, anyway, I'm sure you can handle my garden!" she said warmly. "And if you can get everybody in town to help, it's all right with me!" He giggled at that.

"Would five dollars a week be enough to start with?" she asked.

He gasped. Five dollars was a fortune!

"Y-yes, ma'am!" he managed to stutter.

"All right then. You can start whenever you want to."

"T-tomorrow?"

"Tomorrow's Sunday!" she laughed. "Say Monday after school. I'll see you then."

"Well," he said to Mama and Pearl, sticking out his chest, "guess what, folks! I've got a job!"

CHAPTER **6** THE HAPPIEST DAYS

Early spring was busy and happy on Fourth Place. Mrs. Harlow said she'd never known the folks in the block to be so pleasant and so neighborly. It was true that no one ever saw Mrs. Lubrano, and Mr. Lubrano was not very friendly. Except for the Italian family, the people seemed to like one another better than they ever had. Mrs. Cotter called on Mrs. Harlow, and they both called on Mrs. Anderson, and Mrs. Weinberg entertained all the mothers at her house one day, with bagels and blackberry juice. And, of course, they talked about their children.

After the picture of the dumping party was published in the paper, the people from all over town and up on the hill began coming by in cars. One Sunday Mr. Huntington talked in church about the club and inspired all the church people to walk or drive past the block to see the lot.

As spring came on, Angelo planted a row of flowers all along the sidewalk. Since he had an "Italian green thumb" —Mrs. Weinberg said—the border grew like mad.

But the empty lot wasn't the only place to have its face lifted.

One day in late April—one of those rare days now, when Preston and Benjy had time to stroll along together and talk things over as they used to do—they passed the Andersons' house and saw Peter and Paul on stepladders.

"Well, what do you know!" Benjy exclaimed. "The Andersons are painting their house!"

Murf was coming out just then, on his way to the newspaper office, and he stopped to admire the job.

"What do you think of green for a color?" he demanded.

"Swell!" Preston exclaimed. "Your house is going to look the best on the block."

"I bet somebody comes along and wants to buy it!" Benjy said. "I bet every house on the block gets a chance to be sold."

"How about yours?" Murf asked. "I see the sign's still there."

Benjy said his father hadn't mentioned selling for some time now—but the sign still stayed.

"The landlord furnished the paint," Murf explained. "He said it was worth it to get a free paint job."

"That was lucky for you," Preston said. Then he called up to the twins, "How's the weather up there?" Peter waved his paintbrush, and the boys all dodged to escape a shower of bright green drops that came raining down.

"Looks like the Lubranos have been doing something, too," Benjy commented, as the three went on down the street. "Lookit! Angelo cleaned up around there and planted something in that dirt around the house." He pointed to the freshly dug earth at the edge of the porch.

Benjy whistled, and Mr. Lubrano came to the door.

"Stop hanging around the yard!" he told them sternly. "You drive away customers!"

"Oh, no we won't!" Murf exclaimed. "We'll bring you customers, Mr. Lubrano. People will think we all came to buy something and that your stuff must be pretty good to have so many people buying it."

"Gee, that reminds me!" Benjy said. "My mama wants some oranges. She wants fifty cents' worth."

Mr. Lubrano opened the door reluctantly. He was a little more gracious as he put the fruit into a bag.

"My oranges very tasty!" he remarked proudly.

"Yes, sir!" said Preston. "And your store looks nice, and smells good, too!"

Mr. Lubrano almost smiled. Then his face straightened again, and he said quickly, "Well, well, well, go now, boys. Business is business!"

"Where's Angelo?" Benjy asked.

"Angelo is gone! Angelo is busy! Angelo is not at home!" Mr. Lubrano said quickly.

"How's Mrs. Lubrano?" Preston remembered to ask then.

"My wife is sick," Mr. Lubrano said briefly. "Good-by, boys."

As the boys went on, Benjy remarked about how Mr. Lubrano had almost smiled. "I thought his face was going to crack!" Benjy said.

They laughed, but Preston thought that Mr. Lubrano looked more worried than cross. "Reckon he's got important things to think about," he said to himself, as he left Benjy.

Word had gradually gone around town that the boys were saving for a swimming pool, and of course everybody was interested, although most of them were more amused than believing. Mr. Bigelow of the Bugle said he was holding that story for the "scoop of the year." Mr. Huntington at the church continued to be their strong champion. And Mr. Spriggs at the bank began to watch for Preston's weekly deposits with keen concern. "At last," he said, "I've found boys who can save!"

Over the week end Preston always kept the money in the tin can, hidden in the niche at the foot of the tree, and on Monday he took it to the bank during the noon hour. All the clerks at the bank knew him, but Preston never went to them. He did his business with Mr. Spriggs, and every Monday Mr. Spriggs added a dollar to the deposit!

The boys were as much excited over their rising bank

account as over the celebrated "community betterment." One day Murf brought in a pocket full of nickels and dimes which the people who worked in the newspaper office had collected "for the big project." Murf seemed to be doing well at his job, although he complained a good deal because he had no bicycle. Benjy said he had just as much hiking around to do on his job as Murf did, and he managed without a bike. But Murf declared all paper boys needed bikes.

Preston thought that of all the jobs in town his own was best. The faster the grass grew the better he liked it.

Preston and Mrs. Spriggs usually worked together because Mrs. Spriggs liked the outdoors and was proud of the big garden in back of the house. Sometimes Preston pretended the garden was his own.

"I feel like it sort of is mine," he confided to her one day, when she was setting out flowers and he was digging the little holes to put them in.

Mrs. Spriggs nodded understandingly.

"I think we get to feeling that way about a place where we've worked with our hands," she said. "And April gives us plenty of work to do here, doesn't it?"

A little later, while they were digging together along the brick walk, she spoke so suddenly that he was startled.

"Preston," she said, "I've been wondering for a long time about that swimming pool you boys want. How did you happen to get the idea in the first place?"

He had almost forgotten! But the whole story came out—about how he and Benjy had gone to Metropolis together in February and how they'd come back without going into the pool. Mrs. Spriggs was very thoughtful. At the end of the story she didn't say a word, but she cleared her throat several times and then went into the house. He didn't see her again until he went to the house to say good-by. She patted him on the shoulder, said he'd done a fine job, and handed him an envelope, sealed.

"It's a little contribution for your swimming pool," she explained. "Mr. Spriggs and I are getting as interested in that as you boys, I think!"

Preston was pleased. He tucked the envelope in his trousers pocket without looking inside. It was another dollar, he was sure, because that was what Mr. Spriggs often added to the deposit.

And as he went on home that evening, he whistled the tune they'd learned from Mr. Huntington—the working tune. Life had never seemed quite so pleasant. He had never been happier. He was glad to be alive.

Afterward, when he thought about it, Preston reckoned that April day as the end of the good days. But how could he have known at that moment all that was going to happen?

And yet the next day began just like the other Saturdays.

First of all, it was club meeting day. Everybody was there early except Angelo. While they waited for him, they counted the money, always an exciting part of a meeting. There were three dollar bills and two dollars in change, including one twenty-five cent piece that Murf put in. Benjy said that twenty-five cents was pretty small, considering the big salary Murf got for delivering papers.

"But I've got to buy a bicycle!" Murf explained.

"We'll never get a swimming pool, looks like!" Benjy complained. "You could put in more than a quarter!"

That reminded Preston. "Say, wait a minute!" he exclaimed. "I've got an extra—from Mrs. Spriggs. He took the envelope from his pocket. "She sent a dol—" Then he stopped and stared at the bill he was taking out of the envelope. "Hey!" He looked at it closely.

"Am I blind?" he demanded. "Look at that!"

They looked and gasped. It was a ten dollar bill!

"Gee whiz!" Joe whistled. "That's more than we ever had all at one time!"

Preston's heart turned over. He was thrilled about the money. But he was even gladder about Mrs. Spriggs. She really must be pleased with his gardening, he thought!

"What's the whole amount, Pres?" Joe asked. "How much have we got?"

Preston took out the black bank book and went down the column of figures Mr. Spriggs had written in it. He counted and added carefully, and then on another piece of paper he added the new fifteen dollars.

"We'd have sixty-five dollars and twenty cents, but we

paid four dollars for the truck that time, and so now we've got sixty-one dollars and twenty cents."

Preston made his report proudly.

"Only sixty-one twenty!" Joe said disappointedly. "It'll take a long time to get enough for that pool."

"How much would it cost, do you think?" Murf said. "We ought to have asked somebody about it maybe."

"Mr. Huntington says it may be five hundred dollars, maybe even more," Joe answered. Murf whistled, and Joe went on, "We'll never do it! Here it's practically summer now and seems like we haven't done a thing."

"Maybe you haven't," Benjy snapped, "but the rest of us have all right."

Joe flushed. He was the only one without a job, and although his mother insisted he was needed at home and paid him an allowance for helping her, it wasn't quite the same thing as a real job.

"Well, we've done some other things, too, you know," Preston said quickly. He felt sorry for Joe. "Your father is real pleased, isn't he, Benjy?"

"But he still wants to sell!" Joe reminded them. "The sign is there all right. Your pop just wants us all to work and get things fixed up so he can get a better price!"

"Oh, cut it, fellows," Murf said. "That's a heck of a lot of money, I think! And we've had fun fixing Fourth Place."

"And we've got a good club," Preston added. "Mr. Huntington says this is the best bunch he ever met!"

"Funny how we all felt about Italians before the Lubranos came," Joe remarked suddenly.

"Yeah," Benjy agreed. "And the way Angelo talked about niggers and kikes! Seems like a long time ago. Say, does anybody know where Angelo is?"

Nobody knew.

"Bet his father wouldn't let him come!" Benjy said.

"Maybe it was because he couldn't bring any money," Joe thought. "His mother has to have an operation."

Preston remembered then.

"Pearl saw them leave in a taxi right about breakfast time. They must have gone someplace. Is the shop closed?"

Nobody had noticed about that.

"I'll go around and see," Joe said. "Seems funny!"

Murf went along with Joe because he wanted to go to the store to look at the bicycles. Preston and Benjy were left alone. Preston put the money into his wallet.

"Want to go around home with me to put it away?" he said to Benjy.

When they reached the gray house, they saw Mrs. Harlow beckoning from the window.

Preston waved, but he and Benjy stopped to put the money away before he went inside.

"Fifteen dollars is more than we ever left before," Preston remarked, as he stuffed the can lightly into the niche. "Reckon it's safe?"

"Oh, sure," Benjy said. "We've always put stuff there."

"Yeah—well, so long."

Mama was a little impatient when he went in. "You took a long time," she said. "What were you doing?"

"Oh, nothing," he told her.

But Mama wasn't really thinking about the tree.

"You know, Preston," she said, "I'm worried about the Lubranos."

"Is there something the matter?" he asked. "Why did they leave this morning?"

"Mrs. Lubrano is worse," she said slowly. "Mr. Huntington called today and said she needs to have an operation."

Preston swallowed. "Gee, that's awful," he muttered.

"And—Pressy, they need some money for it. So the neighbors are taking up a little collection."

"Gee!" he exclaimed again. "Will we give some?"

His mother nodded thoughtfully.

"We'll have to cut some corners, but we can do it," she said. "I think five dollars would be a help."

Preston was trying to have a thought that he couldn't quite get hold of. It kept escaping him.

"I—I could do without my new suit this spring," he said.

His mother smiled. "We'll see about the suit."

Later that night Preston began to wonder if he'd spoken too quickly. He was getting too big for his old suit.

Yet there was that thought he was trying to remember! It had to do with money. He went to sleep, wondering what it was that he couldn't quite remember!

Banking day was usually the most exciting time of the week for Preston. He enjoyed the rush home at noon, snatching a bite of lunch, digging out the money from its hiding place, and running all the way to the bank, where he handed over the money to Mr. Spriggs! Being treasurer was a responsible job!

But today it was all different, from the very beginning. He woke up with a feeling of something being wrong, and when he saw Mama standing in the kitchen window looking out toward the Lubrano house, he knew that she was thinking the same thing he was.

"Angelo and his father just left," she said.

"I hope they get enough money for the operation!" he exclaimed.

His feet dragged on the way to school. He forgot all

about stopping at the tree to look at the can as he usually did. All he could think of was the sign on the front of Mr. Lubrano's shop door—"Shut—sickness."

He noticed a bicycle leaning up against Murf's porch, painted bright blue. So Murf had got his bike! But even that didn't seem very important.

All morning long Angelo's empty seat in the third row of the schoolroom reminded him of Mrs. Lubrano and the hospital. He kept thinking, "What if it were Mama!"

At recess the boys gathered in a huddle to talk it over.

"Oh, shucks!" Benjy said pityingly.

"Do you reckon they can get enough money for the operation?" Murf asked.

"My mother says the Catholics ought to do something to help," Joe remarked.

"Mr. Huntington says this is a time for folks to be neighborly," Preston recalled.

"I hope somebody does something!" Benjy exclaimed. "Look at the Spriggses and all the money they've got!"

"And look at all your father's got!" Joe observed.

"Everybody's got more than Angelo!" Preston said.

When Preston started home at noon, he was still thinking of Angelo. Suddenly he remembered it was banking day. He raced all the rest of the way home and gobbled his lunch so fast that Mama was distressed.

"Big hurry!" he mumbled with his mouth full. "It's bank day! 'Bye!" And he was out at the crab apple tree.

He stooped to reach into the niche by the ground, stirring quickly with his hand among the leaves.

But there was something wrong. The can seemed to be buried deeper than he'd remembered. He dug farther, and then a cold feeling swept all over him. He couldn't seem to feel anything except leaves. He dug again and finally got down on his knees to look.

There wasn't any can! There was nothing but leaves!

He stood up, trembling. No can! The money was gone! What should he do?

It must be a bad dream. He moved slowly, dizzily, toward the gate. Who—who had taken the money? Surely he'd put it there in the niche. Benjy knew about the place. And Murf knew. And right there, leaning up against the Andersons' door, he could see Murf's new bicycle.

No, he wouldn't think that, not yet. Anyway, Murf hadn't seen him put the money away the other night. Benjy? Again his heart thumped fast. But no. Not Benjy. He just wouldn't. Somebody else must have found it.

There was no time to tell anybody at school because the last bell was ringing as he ran up the steps. But Benjy seemed to guess that something pretty bad had happened. At recess he rushed over as soon as they were outside.

"What's the matter?" he cried. "You look like somebody died. Is Mrs. Lubrano—"

"No—it's the money!" Preston blurted it out. "That fifteen dollars in the tree. It's gone!"

"Gone?" Benjy stood stock still. "Where'd—are you sure?"

"Yeah. It's gone! I looked for ten minutes."

"But—but somebody must have got it!"

"Looks that way."

"But who—say, did you see Murf's bike?"

"Yeah! Out in front of their house. But the money—"

"Gee! I just wonder!" Benjy began thoughtfully. Before he could say anything more, Murf came striding over to where they were standing.

"What do you look so funny about?" he asked. "Is Angelo's mom worse?"

"No—I don't know," Preston told him. "But—our club money's gone!"

"Gone? Gone where?" Murf demanded. Preston explained.

In two minutes Murf was shouting the word around the playground, and the missing fifteen dollars of the Fourth Place Club was public information! Benjy and Preston, because they'd been the ones to see the money last, seemed to be the suspected ones.

"My mother says it's a mistake mixing with all kinds!" Joe remarked to some of the others, but so that Preston could hear him plainly. "Everybody knows you can't trust a nigger or a Jew."

Benjy and Preston escaped only when the bell rang for the end of recess. All the rest of the afternoon Preston watched the clock on the wall miserably, while he pretended to read. This was the day he had always looked forward to! But now he felt sore all through.

He looked up once to see Benjy staring at him. Did Benjy suspect him? Benjy didn't say so, of course, but— And how about Benjy anyway? He knew about the hiding place! Somebody had taken that money!

When school was over, Preston hurried out as fast as he could and ran down the street without stopping even when he heard a familiar whistle behind him. Benjy caught up before he got very far away.

"Listen, Pres!" he panted. "Listen—don't run off half cocked that way. I never said a word to you!"

"You—you were thinking something bad about me!" Preston retorted.

"You're crazy. What in the world would you want with fifteen dollars when you could get the whole amount in the bank and go to California with it—if you wanted to. I know you didn't take it. And I didn't either. I don't need that fifteen dollars. The only guy that needed it was Murf—except—"

"Joe said he wanted a slice!" Preston remembered.

"Well—" Benjy hesitated. "It doesn't sound like the kind of thing Joe would do. He's stuck-up, but—"

"But what?"

"Angelo needed it for his mother's operation," Benjy said unwillingly.

"But he wasn't even there! He didn't even know there was any money," Preston insisted.

"No. But nobody knows where he was. He might have been home and seen you put it there. Still—"

"I don't think it was Angelo," Preston said.

"Well, what we've got to do is find out who did take it and prove it, that's all. Do you remember how the money was? There was that ten dollar bill you put in. And the rest was in ones, except three quarters and two dimes and a nickel, and two fifty cent pieces. Wasn't that the way it was?"

"Yeah, I guess so," Preston said admiringly. "I couldn't begin to remember that way!"

"Did you see anybody around? Anybody watching?"

"Nobody I know of. Mama was shaking the mop."

Benjy laughed. "Well, she's out! Anybody else but your mother!" he said.

"I should think so!" Preston exclaimed.

"But Pres—" Benjy said, "Pres, I guess we'd better not say anything to your mother about the money, do you think? It would just bother her, wouldn't it?"

Preston nodded miserably.

"I won't say anything," he promised.

"O.K.! Mum's the word! Don't you worry now!" Benjy urged. "Just give us some time, and we'll get that thief!"

Preston found he couldn't go inside the house even after he got there. He looked at the closed front door and at the crab apple tree, holding its secret. Finally he decided to take a walk.

Preston never really knew where he walked that afternoon or how he happened to find himself clear on the other side of town and close to the Catholic church. But suddenly he noticed the dark brick building ahead with its tall iron spire, and it reminded him again of Angelo. Poor kid! He'd almost forgotten Mrs. Lubrano and Angelo, with all his own troubles.

He stopped and stood there looking at the church. So this was where Angelo came on Sundays! Preston had never been inside a Catholic church. Joe had said there were lots of statues and the Catholics prayed to them. If he'd pray about that lost money, would it turn up, he wondered.

"Hi, Pres!" somebody called from behind him.

Preston jumped, turned around, and then stiffened. Of all people in the world for him to meet today this was the limit—Joe Cotter! Well, he said to himself, if Joe thought he was going to take any more of that talk about niggers, he just had another think coming.

But Joe seemed to have something else on his mind that evening.

"What are you doing here?" he asked. His voice sounded a little friendly!

"Nothing," Preston answered. "Just taking a walk. How about you?"

"Just taking a walk, too. Thought I'd come over and see—" he hesitated. "I was thinking about Angelo. I—I just got to thinking."

"He's at the hospital, I guess."

"Yeah, I saw him."

"Did you go to the hospital?" Preston demanded.

"Yeah," Joe said, looking embarrassed. "Mother sent me over. She thought we ought to do something. I was just thinking—"

Preston began to understand. He'd been thinking, too!

"Hey, there he is!" Joe said suddenly. "Coming around the corner on the run."

Sure enough, there was Angelo, a forlorn little figure hurrying along, his thin shoulders hunched.

"Hi, kid!" Joe called.

Angelo, surprised, stopped for a second, and then slowly came on toward them.

"Going in the church?" Joe asked him.

Angelo looked embarrassed.

"I—yeah," he said and moved as if to pass by them.

"How—how's your mother?" Preston asked.

"Bad!" Angelo said shortly. "That's why I've got to do a novena."

"A—a what?"

"You burn a candle while you make a—a—while you ask for something," Angelo explained haltingly.

"Gee—and do you get it?" Joe asked.

"I—I hope so!" Angelo's lip trembled, and he went into the church.

"Certainly is queer," Joe commented. "I never did understand about Catholics. Going home now?"

"I guess so."

"So am I."

Preston wished they needn't go together. He still felt angry with Joe. They walked along for a while without speaking.

"Say, Pres," Joe said finally. It was unusual for him to say "Pres"! "I didn't mean what I said today. Guess it made you mad."

Preston couldn't answer.

"Nobody thinks you took the money," Joe went on. "Or Benjy either. I just got excited."

"That's O.K.!" Preston mumbled at last.

"Angelo's a good kid."

"Sure."

"You know, Pres, I got to thinking today—what if it was my mother in the hospital—"

"Why—why I did, too!" Preston exclaimed in amazement. "I mean I thought what if it was mine!"

They both laughed. It seemed funny for Joe and Preston to have thought the very same thing!

"She's mighty bad, I guess," Joe said then.

When Joe left him, Preston kept wondering about what had happened. He told Mama about it later.

"Why did Joe like Angelo, right from the start, Mama?"
he asked.

"Maybe it's just the way we all are," she suggested. "We
like some people right away. Or maybe Joe felt as if Angelo
might be lonely." She paused and then went on thoughtfully. "Maybe Joe's been lonely, too."

"Well, Joe acted friendly to me today!" Preston said
wonderingly. "I wonder what made him?" He told her
then how he and Joe had had the very same thought!

"I—I guess we were just alike!" he exclaimed.

"You and Benjy haven't always been so nice to Joe, have
you, Preston?"

"He didn't act like he wanted us to."

"Maybe he wanted you to but didn't want you to know
how he felt," she suggested.

Preston thought about that. Then of Angelo.

"You know, Angelo prays in church for things, Mama.
He prays to statues," he said. "And, Mama, he lights a
candle and prays. He says that's a novena."

"Oh?"

"Yes. Do you think praying to statues would make a wish
come true?"

She hesitated.

"It seems to me that statues and things don't make so
much difference," she said slowly. "But I think the wish is
important. And if you wish for what you think is right and
talk to God about it and do your best to help it happen

yourself, that's the best way to make your wishes come true."

"And if that kind of wish comes true, does it mean God answered your prayer, Mama?"

"I think it's that way, Preston," she said.

"Benjy says they pray at the synagogue, too," he said. "Jews and Catholics and us—everybody prays. It's funny, isn't it?"

"It's a good thing to remember!" she said. "You've been troubled about things, haven't you, Pressy?"

He nodded.

"Do you think you could just tell yourself that if you keep hoping and trying and praying, things have a way of working out?"

"Yes'm, I think so!"

"And joy comes in the morning. Remember?"

"Yes'm. G'night," he said.

Preston felt good. In spite of all the trouble of the day, he still felt good!

CHAPTER 8 THE MYSTERY IS
SOLVED

It seemed to Preston and Benjy that Murf must have been the one who took that money! Benjy went to Mr. Carlson's store and by some skillful questioning learned that one of the bills Murf had paid for the bike had been a tenner. The bike, with a new coat of paint, had cost thirteen dollars and fifty cents.

"Now where else would Murf get as much as thirteen dollars and fifty cents at a throw?" Benjy demanded of Preston, in great excitement. "He must be the one!"

"But maybe he saved it up," Preston suggested.

"Not Murf! He can't save up anything!"

Preston knew that. None of the Andersons could hold onto money long enough to get past a candy store.

"Why, you have to practically be there when the newspaper pays him, to get his club money!" Benjy declared.

At that very moment, Murf rode up on the bike and pulled to an impressive stop in front of them. Preston stiffened, ready to hear him say something mean. But Murf seemed to have forgotten what had been said the day before.

"Say, fellows," he cried, "I bet I know what happened to our money!"

"What do you mean?" Benjy asked cautiously.

"I bet it was Joe Cotter! He sure is acting funny. Won't hardly speak!"

"Somehow it—it just doesn't sound like Joe!" Preston said slowly. He remembered about the church.

"He told me once he'd like to have back what he put in. He was mad about something, I think," said Murf.

"Well—" Benjy hesitated. "I feel like Pres. Some way you expect Joe to do something—well big."

"Big? I call this big," Murf exclaimed. "Maybe fifteen dollars doesn't sound like much to you, but—"

"It'll almost buy a bike!" Benjy observed. Murf flushed.

"If you're saying—" he began, doubling up his fists.

"Nobody said anything," Preston put in hastily. Murf sprang onto his bicycle and whirled off.

"I think he's just trying to put it off on Joe," Benjy said thoughtfully. "But if Joe didn't do it, and if Murf didn't do it himself, well that just leaves Angelo, and I'd hate to face him with it right now."

"Yeah, I would, too," Preston said.

Coming home that day was hard. He wanted more than ever to tell Mama about the problem. But he couldn't. Did Mama know? Was she keeping something from him?

But when he got home, Mama called to him cheerfully from the front door. Her voice sounded just the same as usual. Surely nothing was wrong!

"Pressy," she exclaimed, as he came dragging in, "you need cheering up. And I've got the very thing to do it. It's a surprise!"

"Surprise?" He was curious in spite of his worries.

"Look in the box!"

It was a suit box, a big gray one, new and neat, sealed on all four sides.

"For me?" he asked wonderingly.

"For you. And you do need it. It's special!"

Eagerly he tore away the seals and with trembling fingers lifted the lid off the box.

"Mama!" he cried. "It's a new suit! Gray!"

Still trembling, he lifted the coat out of the box. Soft gray wool! He pressed it against his cheek, loving the feel of it. And lined with blue silk! Silk! He laid the coat carefully over the back of a chair and then lifted out the trousers. Slowly, smoothly, they unfolded under his hands.

"Gee, it's swell!" he exclaimed. "It's—it's just the most beautiful suit in the world!"

He rushed to try it on, yanking off his sweater and trousers in a hurry to dive into the new ones. The suit fitted just right, and did he ever look handsome! He pranced joyfully up and down in front of the mirror.

"I feel pretty good about the fit!" his mother observed with satisfaction. "The pants seem to be right, and the coat, too. Maybe a little long in the sleeves."

It was while he was admiring himself in the glass that he remembered. Slowly he turned away from the mirror to look at Mama.

"Something wrong with it?" she asked. "Is it too tight?"

"It's just right," he said. "But—but we can't afford it."

She laughed. Then she was serious.

"Don't worry about the money, Preston."

"How much did it cost?" he insisted.

She handed the price tag to him.

"Thirty-five dollars!" he exclaimed. "But that's a lot! And you said—about Angelo's mother—"

Mama sat down. "Preston," she said earnestly, "maybe we've talked too much about money in this family. I want you to remember that money isn't important except as it can be exchanged for the things people need. There are lots of things you can't get with money. But you can get a suit of clothes. And you need that suit. We'll save on something else. But there's enough for it."

Carefully he took off the new suit and hung it in his closet. It was the most beautiful thing he'd ever owned.

After supper he sat with his book open in front of him, not reading but just thinking, mostly about the money.

Murf had a new bicycle. It had cost thirteen dollars and fifty cents. And he'd got the bicycle Saturday afternoon or Saturday night maybe. But Murf—well he didn't think it was Murf.

Joe had talked about a slice of money. But no, it couldn't have been Joe!

Angelo needed it most of all. And if it had been Preston's mother in the hospital, wouldn't he himself have been tempted? He certainly would have! Did Angelo know about the hiding place?

Benjy? Benjy didn't need money of course. And yet— and yet Benjy knew about the tree. And all of them— except maybe Angelo—knew about the can.

The suit had cost thirty-five dollars, and his family couldn't afford that much. He knew it. But—he stopped thinking that way.

Where had the money gone?

The puzzle grew more and more puzzling.

The days dragged by until Saturday came again, when the club usually held its meeting. Preston hardly thought they'd have one this time, because there didn't really seem to be a club any more. But when Benjy came by, they decided to go on over to the church—from force of habit, as Benjy said. To their surprise, Murf's bicycle was leaning up against the basement door.

"You'd think he'd be able to get this far on his own feet, wouldn't you!" Benjy exclaimed.

Murf was the only one in the club room.

"I didn't think there'd be any meeting, but Joe said he was coming," he explained. "He's got something up his sleeve, looks like. And I got to hurry. Anyway, I don't care about staying around where they think I stole!"

"Oh, gosh, Murf!" Preston couldn't think of anything else to say. Benjy might have, but before he could open his mouth, the door opened again and in came Joe.

After that nobody could say anything. In his hand Joe carried a tin can, with a green plant rooted inside.

"Well I'll—I'll be!" Benjy exploded. "It's our can!"

Preston was dumb.

"The money's in the bottom," Joe said. "Every cent of it." But he held onto the can.

"I don't get it," Murf exclaimed. "How'd you find it?"

"That's for me to know," Joe said shortly. "What I got to say is that the money is here, and I'll give it up to you if you'll promise one thing. If you won't—well I won't give it up, that's all."

"Wh-what do you want to do with it?" Benjy said.

"I want to put it in the collection for Mrs. Lubrano's operation," Joe said.

"But fifteen dollars!" Murf cried. "That's a lot of money!"

"It's not much for an operation," Joe reminded him.

"But it's—it's our money!" Murf protested.

"How about it, fellows?" Joe turned to the others.

"Well—" Benjy hesitated. "I don't think Joe's got a right to keep the money, no matter what."

"What about it, Pres?" Joe still held firmly onto the can. "Can we give it to Angelo?"

Preston's head was swimming. His first feeling was relief so great that it almost made him sick. His second feeling was surprise. So it had been Joe all the time!

Last of all he thought of the hospital. Fifteen dollars for the hospital! But he was trying to think of something else that wouldn't quite come.

Joe was waiting, holding the can.

"I think it's all right to give it for the operation," Preston said suddenly. "Angelo's one of the crowd. But—but—"

"But what?" Joe clung to the can.

"But it's not much for an operation," Preston said slowly. He ought to be able to think of what was in the back of his mind. What was the matter with him?

"It'll help!" Joe said. "Anyway, it's all we've got."

Something clicked. Preston had it at last!

"No, it's not all we've got!" he shouted. "We've got sixty-one dollars and twenty cents. I think we ought to give it all to Angelo."

Benjy and Murf looked dazed. Even Joe looked surprised. And Preston was amazed at himself!

"But—it's our swimming pool!" Murf screeched at last. "What are you talking about? Are you nuts?"

"Pres!" Benjy exclaimed. "Are you feeling all right? Are you sick?"

"No, I'm not sick," Preston said slowly. "I feel like I've just got over being sick though. Listen, fellows! My mother said something. She said money doesn't amount to anything except if you can change it for something somebody needs. We don't really *need* any swimming pool. You know we don't. And let's face it—we couldn't get one for maybe two years anyway. And right now—"

"Right now Angelo's mother will die, maybe, unless she has an operation!" Joe exclaimed. "What if it was your mother?"

Benjy was looking thoughtful, too.

"Yeah," he said. "If it was my mother, and my father didn't have any money— Poor kid! Poor Angelo!"

"Come on, Murf!" Preston begged. "You got a bike. And you got a job. And—gee, it's his mother. Look at the way he planted those flower seeds around the lot!"

"O.K.," Murf said finally. "I don't care what you do with it. I guess we couldn't get that pool anyway, like Pres said."

"Then that settles it," Benjy said briskly. "And if we'd thought of it last week, we'd have saved ourselves a lot of trouble!"

"I bet we can pay for the whole operation!" Murf exclaimed. "Sixty-one dollars! That's a fortune!" He looked at Joe. "Let me see that can, fellow!"

"Pres is the treasurer!" Joe said, handing the can to Preston. "He can count it."

Preston reached inside the can cautiously, to take out the plant. What a funny little thing it was! He felt down under the dirt. The false bottom was there. And— yes—there was the envelope. As he pulled it out, damp from the dirt, a fifty cent piece rolled out on the table. Murf stopped it from falling on the floor. Preston dumped the rest of the heap, including the damp ten dollar bill.

"Fifteen bucks!" Benjy counted quickly.

"Say how come you started planting flowers, Joe?" Murf asked.

"None of your business, smart guy!" Joe answered tartly. "Is it all there, Pres?"

"Gee, yes. Thanks, Joe!" Preston murmured and began planting the flower back in the can.

"Thanks?" Murf exclaimed. "What do you mean— thanks? It's not Joe's money!"

"I'll get the rest out of the bank on Monday so we can give it to the collection," Preston said quickly. No use for Murf to keep nagging at Joe that way.

But Joe didn't seem to care what Murf said. He had something else on his mind.

"Pres," he said earnestly, "listen! I just want to tell you you're the best kid in Mayville!"

"Well—gosh!" Preston said.

"And—fellows!" Joe went on. "While I'm saying it I—

well, I'm going to say it, that's all. This is a great club! It's the only club I ever heard of like it, and—well, I think we ought to go ahead and be the first club in town to have a Negro for a president. That's what I think!"

"That's what I said in the first place!" Benjy reminded him.

"I think it's a good club, too," Murf said. "And I—well, I don't mind giving up that money. I'm glad to. It makes you feel real good!"

Benjy remarked that since they had the money matters settled, they might as well go on about their business, and with the meeting over, they all walked home together, Murf wheeling his bicycle along beside Preston. A real club again! It seemed as though suddenly there was more to say than they'd ever had to say before.

By the time they reached the gray house, they were so busy talking they might have passed on by if they hadn't met Mama coming from the store.

"Something special today?" she asked.

"Certainly is!" Murf exclaimed. "We found the money, Mrs. Harlow. Joe had it!"

"What money?" Mama looked at Preston. Before he could speak, Benjy began blurting out the whole story, with Murf interrupting here and there. She looked astounded.

"So here came Joe with the can, and we're going to give all our money to Angelo!" Benjy concluded.

"Well!" she exclaimed. "That really is a story!"

"And we don't know who took the money!" Benjy explained.

"It was Joe, wasn't it?" Murf insisted. "I don't mean I'm mad or anything, but I thought it was Joe! Of course, he brought it all back so it's O.K.," he added.

Joe didn't say a word. But Mama laughed and patted him on the shoulder.

"No, it wasn't Joe!" she said. "I think I can tell you who the thief was. I'm afraid it was Preston's mother!"

"Wh-what?" Benjy shrieked. Preston gasped. Joe and Murf stood with mouths open. Mama laughed again.

"Oh, dear, if you'd only told me what was bothering you, Preston! I couldn't think what was the matter!" Then she explained. "You see I was raking leaves under the tree, and I saw the top of the can poking through. I meant to throw it into the trash can, but Angelo came along looking for something to plant a flower in for his mother—and the tin can looked like the very thing. We put some more dirt in on top of what was there. That's all."

"I found the can on Angelo's porch, with the plant in it!" Joe cried. "I found it after all the row Monday. I wasn't going to tell you, because Angelo didn't know it was our can. I know he didn't. And there was the money in the bottom. He just wanted to plant a flower!"

"So you took all the blame yourself!" Murf said wonderingly.

"Joe, you're some guy!" Benjy exclaimed.

Joe laughed and looked embarrassed.

"It's O.K.," he said. "You took some nagging yourself, Murf, about your bike."

"Yeah," Murf laughed. "But I'll tell you how I got that bike if you'll promise to keep mum."

Preston gasped, and Murf went on cheerfully. "It was the men at the newspaper office. They've been looking for a bargain for me, and when this turned up, well, they loaned me the money. I'm going to pay back some on it every week. I wasn't going to tell that because they never did it before, and Mr. Bigelow said to keep it under my hat. Don't you guys tell, now."

"Well!" Benjy whistled. "This is the funniest thing I ever heard!"

Preston couldn't say anything. Life was too wonderful.

There was just one other question on his mind. He could ask Mama now, and did, just as soon as the boys were gone.

"Where did you get enough money for my new suit?" he asked her bluntly.

"Well"—she hesitated—"you had your secret, so I had mine, too. It was a little nest egg I'd been saving out of the money from your father's insurance. It wasn't in a tin can, but while you were saving for a swimming pool, I was saving for the suit. It's becoming to you, too!"

He didn't say any more for fear he might cry.

CHAPTER 9 THREE GREAT DAYS

The month of June was the best of the year for the Fourth Place Club, and there were three days of that month that stood out as the very best of all. The first of the big days was the second of June, when they all went to the bank to get the money out for Mrs. Lubrano's operation.

Preston thought it was important that they should all go and do it together. Murf and Joe weren't too eager to go with him, for they were somewhat in awe of the bank, but Benjy was ready, and in the end they all made the trip. Mr. Spriggs was surprised to see the whole crowd coming in, but as usual he stood up and greeted Preston cordially.

"Well!" he said. "This must be an occasion!"

"Yes, sir, it's an occasion!" Preston laughed.

"Good! Come on inside."

The others followed Preston through the little gate.

"And now how much money do you have for me today?" Mr. Spriggs asked. "I assume it's a good deal, if it took the whole membership to bring it!"

The other boys didn't know whether he was teasing or not, but Preston knew. He laughed again.

"We *have* got a lot!" he exclaimed. "Fifteen dollars this time!" Mr. Spriggs whistled. "But we're not going to put it in. We want to take all the rest out!"

Mr. Spriggs sat down in his chair and looked grave.

"Take it out?" he asked. "All of it?"

"Every cent of it!" Benjy put in.

"But what about the swimming pool? Are you ready to start on it?" Mr. Spriggs asked.

"No, sir," Preston said. "We changed our minds. We're going to do something else with it."

"Does your mother know about this?" asked Mr. Spriggs. "Does Mr. Weinberg know?" He looked at Benjy. Both Benjy and Preston nodded.

"Well," Mr. Spriggs said at last, "it's yours. I suppose I can't say anything. But I was beginning to think we'd found some boys who really wanted to save!"

He walked over to the section of the bank where the tellers stood at the windows, shaking his head as he walked.

"Do you suppose we ought to tell him?" Murf asked.

"I think we ought to," Benjy said. "After all, he put some in, didn't he?"

"Yes, and Mrs. Spriggs did, too," Preston said. "You tell him, Benjy."

Mr. Spriggs came back with a handful of crisp new bills. "Want an envelope to put it in?" he asked.

"That'll be fine," Preston said. "We can put this other fifteen in, too. That makes sixty-one dollars and twenty cents."

Mr. Spriggs handed Preston the money, saying, "I guess since you earned it, you've got the right to throw a party if you want to." Preston nudged Benjy.

"Mr. Spriggs," Benjy said, swallowing, "we're not going to throw a party. We—we're going to give the money to Mr. Huntington for Mrs. Lubrano's operation."

Mr. Spriggs had been about to dismiss them, but he sat down suddenly.

"You—you're what?" He shouted this time, and some of the clerks in the windows looked over curiously.

"We decided it wasn't enough for a swimming pool anyway," Benjy explained.

"And maybe it isn't much for an operation either, but it might help, and Angelo's in the club—" Joe continued.

Mr. Spriggs seemed unable to speak, but at last he said slowly, "I never thought I'd live to see the day when a bunch of kids—say, who gave you the idea?"

"Nobody," Preston said, but Joe added quickly, "It was Preston. He thought of it."

"Joe made me think of it!" Preston insisted.

Mr. Spriggs let them go at last, and as they went out through the door they saw him pick up his telephone.

"Well, let's get over to the church before we lose the money," Benjy said cheerfully. "We gave him a surprise, looked like!"

Mr. Huntington wasn't sitting in the church office as they had expected. He was standing in the doorway, and he looked almost as if he were watching for them.

"This is an honor!" he exclaimed. "And how are things going with the Fourth Place Club?"

"O.K.," Benjy said. "We've got some important business!"

"Good. Come in and sit down!"

They filed in and sat down around the desk, just like grownups for a meeting.

"What's the business on hand?" Mr. Huntington asked.

"It's about the money for Mrs. Lubrano's operation," Preston said. "We want to—to give some."

Mr. Huntington nodded approvingly.

"That's fine!" he exclaimed. "It'll be appreciated. I've been over to the hospital this morning, by the way. Brought Mr. Lubrano and Angelo back home for a while."

"Is—is she any better?" Murf asked.

"She'll get well," Mr. Huntington said, "if she can have the operation sometime soon."

"We've got our money here," Preston told Mr. Huntington. "It's in this envelope."

Mr. Huntington opened the envelope slowly.

"But—but this is a lot of money!" he exclaimed.

"Sixty-one bucks!" Murf exclaimed.

"But—but you must have brought all you have!"

"That's all of it," Benjy said. "I hope it's enough."

"This is your swimming pool!" exclaimed Mr. Huntington. "Are you boys sure you want to do this?"

"Yes, sir," Joe said quickly. "We're sure, all right!"

Mr. Huntington laid the envelope on the table. He hesitated. Then he smiled.

"This is a magnificent gift!" he said slowly. "The swimming pool—the whole swimming pool—that you've worked for all spring."

Preston looked at the floor. He felt strange. He felt the way he felt in church sometimes. The other boys were silent. Maybe they felt that way, too!

"But, boys"—Mr. Huntington went on at last—"I don't want you to put this money into the collection. This is special. I want you to write your names on the envelope—every one of you—and take it over to Mr. Lubrano yourselves. Will you do that?"

"He might not like it," Preston said.

"He'll like it!" Mr. Huntington assured him.

"We—we're kind of scared of Mr. Lubrano," Murf explained. "He doesn't want us to come around there. Says it drives away business."

"He'll like this!" Mr. Huntington said. "Mr. Lubrano

just doesn't understand about you boys. Will you do it, fellows?"

He offered Preston his pen. Hesitating, Preston took it, wrote his name on the envelope, and then handed the pen to Benjy. One by one, they all signed their names.

"We ought to put Angelo's on, too," Joe reminded them. "It's partly his."

He wrote it in big letters—"Angelo Lubrano."

"And now you take it over there right away, will you?" Mr. Huntington urged them.

He stood watching as they went slowly down the street.

They weren't so sure about going to see Mr. Lubrano, and every step of the way grew a little harder.

"What if he won't even take it?" Murf suggested.

"Then we'll put it back in the bank," Benjy said. "But I think he will."

The fruit store still had its sign "Shut—sickness" in front. When Joe knocked on the door, there was no answer at first.

"You take the money, Joe!" Preston whispered, while they waited. "He doesn't like Negroes!"

"No, sir, you're the treasurer, and it was your idea!" Joe said emphatically. When the door finally opened a crack, he shoved Preston forward. Benjy and Murf, suddenly shy, hung back.

Mr. Lubrano was peeping through the crack.

"The store is shut today," he said. "There is sickness."

"We don't want to buy anything," Preston began.

"Then go away!" said Mr. Lubrano.

"Hey, how's Mrs. Lubrano?" Murf said suddenly.

"Bad, very bad," Mr. Lubrano said. "What do you want, boys? Why don't you go away? You can't see Angelo today!"

"We didn't come to see Angelo," Preston said. "We brought this envelope. It's from the club. It's for the operation."

He handed the envelope to Mr. Lubrano, who seemed not to understand. At last he took it gingerly. Slowly he read all their names, ending with Angelo's.

"What is this?" he asked.

"There's some—well, some money," Preston explained. "It—it's all we had."

"It's because Angelo is in our club," Benjy added in a friendly way.

Mr. Lubrano looked dazed, but he pushed the door open wide and motioned them to come inside. Then slowly he lifted the flap of the envelope. Out came the beautiful crisp new bills from the bank, and with them the damp bills and the change.

"It's sixty-one dollars and twenty cents," Preston explained. "It's for the operation. It's all we had."

What was the matter? Had they done wrong? Was Mr. Lubrano mad? Why didn't he do something? Why didn't he say something?"

Then the strangest thing happened. Mr. Lubrano's face puckered up, and the tears began to run right down his cheeks. The boys were embarrassed.

At last Mr. Lubrano spoke, as if it were hard for him.

"For—for the operation!" he said. "For—Mama!"

Mr. Lubrano looked at Preston, and then, with the tears still running down his face, he looked at the others.

"This is the Jew boy!" he murmured. "And the Negro boy! And the white boys!"

He turned toward the door in the back of the room. "Angelo," he shouted. "Come quick!" He banged his fist on the counter. "Come, Angelo, to see your friends!"

Angelo came running. When he saw the boys, he stopped. But Mr. Lubrano reached for his elbow and drew him firmly over toward the counter.

"Angelo, my son!" he shouted again. "These boys—these good boys—brought money for Mama!" Then he said something in Italian, and Angelo answered. They talked back and forth for a minute or two, with Angelo getting more and more excited and Mr. Lubrano looking more and more amazed. It was funny how fast Italian seemed to go! Mr. Lubrano didn't seem to remember many English words except "White boys, Negro boys, Jew boys," but he said those over and over. And Angelo's eyes sparkled.

"Angelo," Mr. Lubrano said, speaking slow, careful English words so that they could understand, "these are your friends! You are the friend of these boys! Every day you play with them. They have banan—they have orange. Everything in this store you give your friends—hear?"

"Yes, Papa," Angelo spoke at last. Turning to the boys he said, "Gosh—you fellows gave the swimming pool for Mama!"

"The swimming pool!" Mr. Lubrano repeated after him. They both seemed awed.

The boys looked at one another bewilderedly, and then they all laughed. Murf was the one who finally said it.

"This is better than the swimming pool!" he exclaimed.

"This is a lot better!" Benjy cried.

Preston and Joe looked at each other as they trooped

away from the fruit stand. And Preston knew that Joe was feeling the same way that he was! It was a good feeling to end the day with—the first important red letter day of June!

But the second big day, which came about two weeks later, was a red letter one, too. That day Mrs. Lubrano came home from the hospital.

Everybody in the neighborhood came to call for a few minutes. Mr. Huntington called, and Mr. and Mrs. Weinberg called, and of course Mrs. Harlow, and even Mrs. Cotter. As she said, there was something about having gotten together to help a neighbor in an emergency that made everybody feel neighborly. Even the Andersons came—the whole big family.

Rosanne Cotter and Pearl Harlow both came with the Anderson girls, and Preston was amazed to see them all flying about the house, helping Mrs. Lubrano.

"We decided if we didn't have money to give for the operation, we could help her at the house," Pearl explained. "It was Mama that thought of it. Rosanne fixed the flowers, and we all did things. We're kind of a club, too!"

"Well, I'll have to admit girls are some good!" Benjy said generously. "I never thought of helping that way."

"Boys never do," Rosanne said loftily. "All they think of is money, money, money!"

"It comes in handy," Joe reminded her.

Just then Mr. Lubrano came to draw them into the circle around the table.

Mr. Lubrano couldn't seem to do enough for the boys. Preston knew it wasn't because they'd given so much money. All the rest of the people had helped, too. It was because they were "Angelo's friends."

It was the first time they'd had a chance to talk to Mrs. Lubrano, because she'd been sick so much, and Preston decided to his surprise that she was quite a lot like Mama. Angelo showed them pictures of his two little sisters in Metropolis. They were coming home to stay as soon as his mother was up and around again, he said.

Most of all, the boys were fascinated with sitting around the big square dining room table, with its fancy crocheted tablecloth and the big glass fruit bowl in the center. Angelo had been right about the inside of their house, where they lived. It was fine!

Mr. Lubrano urged them to eat all the bananas they could hold, and Mrs. Lubrano promised they'd have a real Italian spaghetti supper when she got into the kitchen.

And the third important day in June?

Well, the third day came a week later, almost. It was really, in a way, Mr. Huntington's day. It was heralded by a notice in the paper saying that Mr. Huntington would like to have a meeting of the whole community in the Central Church, and he wanted everybody—everybody—to be there. The notice was in big block letters set in a frame. The day of the meeting was Friday, and the time was 7:30. The only question was WHAT WAS GOING TO HAPPEN?

CHAPTER 10 THE SWIMMING POOL

W hat could that meeting be for? Preston and Benjy couldn't imagine. But there was one thing sure. It must be special!

"I bet it's com-community betterment!" Murf suggested. They all laughed because Murf always had trouble with big words.

"I bet so, too," Preston agreed. "Mr. Huntington is always talking about that!"

But Mr. Huntington wouldn't explain. He just grinned and told them to be sure to be on hand. All week long the boys became more and more curious. The grownups were curious, too.

Benjy said his father and mother were both coming to the meeting although they never had gone to anything at the church before.

Joe said his mother would be there, too. "She says there's a lot goes on at the church that she doesn't like, but she doesn't want to miss anything!"

Preston asked Mama if he could put on his new suit, and she agreed that this occasion was exactly the right time to wear it.

At long last Friday evening came!

Apparently the whole community thought it was going to be special, just as the people on Fourth Place did, because they were all there. Preston wondered if the church could possibly be big enough to hold them all, as they kept coming and coming. All the people he knew were there, and a great many he'd never seen.

Of course all of Fourth Place had come. The Weinbergs and the Andersons, taking up a whole row, and the Cotters, and—he looked again to be sure—even Mr. Lubrano and Angelo were there, right in Central Church!

Angelo and Benjy were both dressed up in their best, and Preston rather wished there weren't quite so many people because he was afraid his new suit might not show. He felt very proud walking up the aisle with Mama and Pearl, and picking out seats for them, and then waiting just like a grown-up man, while they walked in first. Just the way Mr. Spriggs did when he and Mrs. Spriggs came in.

The Spriggses saw them the first thing and came right down to the front where they were sitting.

"Hello, Preston!" Mrs. Spriggs exclaimed. "And how do

you do, Mrs. Harlow? Are these seats empty?" Mrs. Spriggs sat right down beside Mama.

"I want to tell you that you have a fine young son, Mrs. Harlow!" she said. "We've been working together this spring, and you must come over soon to see our garden!"

Mama's eyes shone as she shook hands with Mrs. Spriggs and Mr. Spriggs, too.

"Your son's a fine businessman, too!" Mr. Spriggs assured her. "I want him in the bank with me some day!"

In just a minute they were all talking away, and Mrs. Spriggs was telling Mama about her favorite kind of rose bush and Mama told her about ordering seeds from Chicago.

Mr. Huntington seemed to be everywhere, saying hello to people and helping them to find seats. Finally, when everybody had come and the doors were shut, he went up in front and stood near the pulpit. Then, although it wasn't Sunday, the whole room hushed.

"It's good to see you here!" he exclaimed. "And it shows the power of the press!" He grinned at Mr. Bigelow, the newspaper editor, who was sitting three seats from the Harlows with a notebook sticking out of his pocket. "That's one of the wonderful things about a community where people know one another. When we have important things to talk over, we can get together to do it! In so many ways I keep being reminded that Mayville is the nicest town I've ever lived in!"

There was a little murmur all through the audience. Mr. Bigelow took his notebook and pencil out of his pocket, but he didn't write anything.

"Even in Mayville," Mr. Huntington went on, "this has been an unusual year. A great many things have happened. Most of us know a little about them but not everything. It seems to me the time has come for us to get together and talk them over. It seems to me it's a good time to talk them over with God, too. Will you pray with me?"

The room was perfectly still while Mr. Huntington prayed, but Preston couldn't help peeping to see how the Lubranos and all of them were doing it. They had their heads bowed, just like everyone else. Maybe they liked to pray in his church, too!

After the prayer, Mr. Huntington didn't say anything. He acted as if he were waiting. Finally he looked over at Mr. Lubrano and smiled. And then, slowly, as if it was hard for him to do it, but as if he wanted to, too, Mr. Lubrano stood up. Everybody turned in amazement to look at him.

"I gotta something to tell everybody!" Mr. Lubrano said. "I tella the preacher I gotta something to say to this town. I gotta lot to say. I wanna say my wife is better. I wanna say thanks to everybody!"

There was another little murmur, and somebody clapped softly. But Mr. Lubrano wasn't through. He swallowed and then went on speaking, fast this time, and more brokenly. The words jumped out.

"I gotta lot more to say!" he exclaimed. "I don't talka the English so good. I gotta the leetle fruit store, and I sella the banan, the apple, all good, all cheap. I gotta something to say. I gotta tell everybody. I tella the preacher" —he paused for breath and then hurried on—"when I come to this town, I no lika nobody. I justa sella the fruit and that's all. I tella my wife, I tella my leetle Angelo, sitting here, 'Donna talka to nobody!' I tella, 'People here you sella the fruit to—you don't talka none.' And my wife she bad seek. Gotta have operation. I no gotta money, sella fruit. No money. No operation. My wife she go to hospital. I walk up and down. I walk up and down! What I gonna do? One day preacher come to buy the banan. He say, 'Whatta wrong, Mr. Lubrano? You seeka man?' I tella my wife is the seeka one. Preacher tella people. Church people gonna help. But that ain't all—

"Whatta happen? Leetle Jew boy and leetle colored boy —alla leetle boys come with envelope. I looka inside. Sixty-one dollars and twenty cents for the operation. I wanna tella everybody—theesa the besta town in the world, and they gotta besta boys. I wanna my leetle boy grow up in theesa town!"

He sat down and wiped his forehead with a handkerchief. For a second there wasn't a sound. Then suddenly everybody clapped and clapped.

Finally Mr. Huntington held up his hand.

"Thank you, Mr. Lubrano," he said. "We think you and your family are good neighbors, too, and we're glad you've come to Mayville. And now folks, Mr. Lubrano has stolen a little of my thunder, but I've got a little more to say. I've got a story to tell you."

Preston pricked up his ears. He had a feeling—

Mr. Huntington was talking about two boys who had gone swimming. And how one of them wasn't allowed to swim because his skin was dark. And how the other boy wasn't willing to go swimming without his friend, and the two had come back on the bus from Metropolis with their dry swimming trunks still folded up. Preston felt Mama's hand reach for his and cling to it tightly.

He'd never heard a room grow so still. There wasn't a

sound except Mr. Huntington's voice. He wasn't speaking in a loud voice either, just quietly as if he were sitting in somebody's front room. But everybody heard every word!

He told how the boys in the neighborhood had decided to dig a hole and make a pool for themselves where they could *all* swim. When Mr. Huntington said that, about digging a hole, there was a little chuckle around the room. Preston saw Mr. Bigelow writing fast in his notebook now!

Being natural boys, Mr. Huntington said, of course they didn't worry because it was a big, expensive job. They just started in earning money and saving it.

"But these boys had another idea, too," Mr. Huntington went on. "And in some ways this seemed more important to them, and it does to me, than the swimming pool. They wanted to do something to make their neighborhood the kind people would enjoy living in and be proud to stay in!" Mr. Huntington looked at Mr. Weinberg, when he said that. "Well," he said, "they got to work, and I think you people will agree with me that Fourth Place is a better looking street than it's ever been—at least in my memory!"

He paused just long enough to take a breath, but before he could begin again there was a rustle in the pew where the Weinbergs were sitting. Mr. Weinberg was jumping up! Preston heard Mrs. Weinberg gasp. Benjy looked scared!

"Excuse me, sir!" Mr. Weinberg shouted, right out in that big crowd of people!

"I didn't expect to make a speech!" he exclaimed. "But I'm just like Mr. Lubrano. I've got to! The little Jew boy he told you about is my boy Benjy, and the little colored boy he told about is his friend Preston, and I want to tell everybody that Fourth Place is a better street than it ever was in my memory, too, and I've lived here longer than anybody. And if you go by my house tonight there will not be a For Sale sign because I'm not going to move. And my lot isn't for sale either. It is not for anybody but the boys. They can have it to use as long as they want to. And whoever comes, I say, 'Welcome to Fourth Place!' It's a good place to live!"

Mr. Weinberg sat down, wiping his forehead as Mr. Lubrano had done.

"Well, thank you, Mr. Weinberg!" Mr. Huntington said then. "The boys will thank you, too, when I give them a chance. But I've got more to say." And to the audience, "You haven't forgotten that swimming pool, have you?"

Preston had forgotten, but the audience hadn't. Mr. Huntington told them then how the boys had worked to raise the money and had put their money in the bank and saved the great sum of sixty-one dollars and twenty cents.

"You've heard what Mr. Lubrano said about the envelope," he said at last. "Well—the money in that envelope —the money the boys brought to help with the operation— that was the Fourth Place Club's swimming pool!"

There was a long silence then. Preston could hear his

own heart thumping, it was so still in the big room. But Mr. Bigelow kept right on scribbling in his book!

Mr. Huntington waited. He looked all around. Preston saw Mr. and Mrs. Spriggs looking at each other. Mrs. Spriggs nodded. Then Mr. Spriggs stood up.

"I'm not a speaker either!" he began. The audience chuckled. "Bankers don't do much speaking. But I've been in on this swimming pool from the beginning and have had the honor of receiving the money from the treasurer here, ever since February!" He smiled down at Preston, and Preston's heart practically stopped beating. "Mrs. Spriggs and I have watched the boys working, and we've seen what's happened on Fourth Place. And—well this business has us by the heart!" There was a murmur in the audience.

"I just want to say," he went on, "that it seems to me they've shown us the way. A swimming pool *is* a good idea. We ought to have one, and it ought to serve the whole community, and I think the whole community ought to work with the boys to get one. Why don't we let them lead us, since they've proved they can do it?" He paused. There wasn't a sound, and he went on. "Here's my proposition. If these youngsters want to start over again, and if the community will guarantee ten dollars for every dollar the boys can put in, I'll match the same dollar with another ten. We aren't millionaires in this town, but we can afford a swimming pool for our young people. What do you say we ask these fine boys to start us all off this year on another community betterment program—the new Mayville swimming pool?"

Mr. Spriggs sat down then and wiped *his* forehead, while Mrs. Spriggs patted him on the shoulder.

For a long time there wasn't a sound. People were thinking hard. Preston looked over at Benjy, and Benjy made the motion of handshaking. Then there was a little whisper around. Finally—of all people—Mrs. Cotter stood up!

"I—I don't know whether or not this is in order," she said hesitatingly, "but I want to move that we undertake this project, if the boys want to do it. Our community certainly isn't rich, but I guess most of our trouble here is that we haven't the kind of courage our children have! I just want to say that my Joe has been happier this spring than I've ever seen him. I want to register my vote for the swimming pool!"

Things happened so fast then that Preston felt his head buzzing as he tried to look around and keep up with who was saying what. Several people shouted, "Second the motion!" and then, instead of voting, like a business meeting, the whole big crowd of people just stood up and cheered. It was like a ball game!

When at last things were quieter, Mr. Huntington pounded on the table and spoke. "Does anybody else want to make a speech?"

Everybody laughed, but nobody volunteered. Then somebody called out from the back, "Let's hear from the

Fourth Place boys!" "Bring them up in front!" somebody else shouted. "Let's have a look at the club!"

Mr. Huntington nodded and began looking around, seeking out the boys.

For a moment Preston felt paralyzed. Then he saw Joe standing up slowly on one side of the church, and Benjy on the other side. Then Murf and Peter and Paul. And Angelo, with his father pushing him firmly out of the seat!

"Come on to the front!" Mr. Huntington insisted. Sheepishly they all walked down the aisle and stood in a line beside him.

"Which one of you is president of the club?" Mr. Huntington asked. Preston began to answer in a small voice that they didn't have one. But the boys were all looking at him! And it was Joe who said, "Preston is! He's the one that started it!"

Mr. Huntington reached his hand toward Preston, and Benjy whispered, "He wants to shake hands, Pres. Stick out your paw!" Weakly, Preston obeyed.

"In the name of the Central Church and the Mayville community," Mr. Huntington said gravely, "I want to give your club our thanks, Mr. President. Your community is back of you. Do you boys want to lead us in getting a swimming pool for Mayville?"

Preston couldn't answer. He couldn't say a word!

It was Murf Anderson who finally spoke up, so that everybody in the whole room heard.

"Sure we want to," he said. "Just so it's for all the kids!"

"Everybody!" Joe added.

"I'm sure that's what your community wants," Mr. Huntington reassured him. "Something for 'all the kids.'"

"And that means *all!*" Mr. Weinberg shouted.

The audience cheered.

"Girls, too!" Benjy declared. The audience clapped again.

"Do you want to make a speech, Mr. President?" Mr. Huntington asked Preston.

Preston looked at Mr. Huntington. Then he looked at the boys. Then he looked at Mama. Her eyes were shining —and yes, she was—Mama was crying, like Mr. Lubrano!

There was a great white flash of light, and he jumped.

"Hey, they're taking our picture!" Benjy whispered. "Say something right quick, Pres!"

"Thank you," Preston began haltingly. Then his legs stopped trembling and at last he grinned right out at that big crowd of people.

"We'll see you at the swimming pool!" he said.

A WORD ABOUT THE FORMAT

This book was set on the Linotype in Electra, an original type face designed by the late W. A. Dwiggins. Because it was drawn to avoid the extreme contrast of thick and thin elements that mark most modern faces, it provides a new type-texture for book composition. Its inherent charm of design has made it one of the most popular of modern faces.

The book was composed and printed by the Sowers Printing Company, Lebanon, Pennsylvania. It was bound by Book Craftsmen Associates, Inc., New York. The jackets and paper covers were printed by offset lithography by Affiliated Lithographers, New York. The text paper is S. D. Warren's Olde Style Laid.

Typographic design by Margery W. Smith
Binding by Louise E. Jefferson